SNATCHES

WENDY VEGA

D1716001

outskirtspress
DENVER, COLORADO

Outskirts Press, Inc.
http://www.outskirtspress.com

ISBN: 978-1-4787-5259-2

Outskirts Press and the "OP" logo are trademarks belonging to Outskirts Press, Inc.

PRINTED IN THE UNITED STATES OF AMERICA

This book is dedicated to Carrie Fisher.
Thanks for the Postcards.

VILLAGE FRIENDS

9/7/58

Dear Diary,

Today was my first day at Village Friends in Greenwich Village. I hope I fit in, but it doesn't look good.

My teacher, Rose, is a beatnik. She speaks softly and wears black. Today she began third grade by arranging us in a circle.

"Hello, class, and welcome. Let's state our names, goals, and which of our parents is blacklisted. I'll go first. I'm Rose. My goal is to teach you about Soviet politics and propaganda techniques. My parents were run over by a beer truck on the Grand Concourse while changing a flat. Next?"

There were thirty kids in the circle, most of whom knew each other from second grade. What to do? Mom says a dry sense of humor will make me popular, and once I learn what that means, maybe I'll develop one. Meantime, I tried to impress my new chums with my spelling.

"Hi. My name is India. My IQ is 165 and I can spell antidisestablishmentarianism."

"Hah, you don't even know what it means!" yelled a swarthy boy. "You're a liar!"

"Of course I don't know what it means. I'm eight! But I can *too* spell it. A-n-t-i...."

Rose jumped in. "Now Stuie, if she says she can spell it,

she can."

"Yeah, well, I can spell it, too. I-T!"

I dislike kids. Of course, I hate myself the most.

"What does she think, we're seniors or something? We don't care about big words. And what kind of pumpkinhead name in India, anyway? Did her mom use an atlas instead of a baby name book? Hahaha!"

"You'll get your turn, Stuie", said Rose. "I think India is a beautiful name."

Rats! I hope I don't become the teacher's pet. The other kids will hate me for sure. If I were Jewish like everyone else, I know they'd like me better, so I decided to lie.

"My goal is to become a more observant Jew."

The circle turned ugly. Shouts of 'Hey, you can't be Jewish with a name like Kelly. I bet you'd don't even know what a bar mitzvah is!' filled the room like small arms fire, causing tears of shame to roll down my cheeks. How could these stupid kids tell I wasn't Jewish? What is a bar mitzvah, anyway? Oy!

"Excuse me Rose, may I say something?"

A voice cut through the din, and I looked up to see a small, red haired boy smiling at me.

"Yes, Arnie, what is it? It's nearly time for Current Communist Events."

"I think everyone is being too hard on India. If she says she's Jewish, I believe her."

Diary, I'm in love! I smiled back gratefully, thankful to have a friend in this hellhole. Arnie Cohen. How I love his name. India Cohen would be better.

Rose rapped her pointer against the blackboard.

"Okay, class, time to move on. This circle thing is definitely not working. So much for emulating the Quakers. Now about those Communists..."

Arnie walked over after class.

"Gee, Arnie, thanks for defending me today."

"It was nothing."

"Yes it was. How come you did?"

"I just don't like when people prosecute each other. It reminds me of the Holocaust."

"I think you mean persecute."

"Right. So, are you really Jewish?"

"Of course not. Do I look like a Jew?"

"Maybe the nose. So how come you said you were?"

"Because everyone else is, even you, and I felt left out. Not even one of my parents is blacklisted, though mom has a photo of the Rosenbergs on her desk. Are you mad?"

"Nah. I'm thinking of becoming an analyst when I grow up."

"And?"

"And you seem like a good kid. A bit neurotic, but all in all, okay. I understand your feelings of self-doubt. Just hang in, and I'll be there if you need to talk. That'll be five bucks."

"The check is in the mail."

"That's what they all say. See you later, Ind."

In my dreams. I guess this school isn't so bad after all. As long as Arnie is on my side, I feel somewhat hopeful. In fact, from here on, I'm gonna name you Hope, dear diary. It sounds more mature, and after all, I'm in third grade now. Love, Me

4/23/59

Dear Hope,

I had a sleepover at Marci's last night, and a weird thing happened while we were bathing. I'm not sure why we bathe together. There's no drought and the Greenbergs are rich, yet Marci always suggests communal baths. I have a huge crush on her brother, Harry, and I keep hoping he'll walk in on us, accidently on purpose. Not that he'd get much of an eyeful at this point, but I can dream. For some reason,

Marci likes washing me.

"India, does it feel good when I wash certain parts of your body?"

"What do you mean by good?"

"Does it feel tingly at all?"

"No, absolutely not. No tingling at all. Why?"

"Oh, nothing. It's just that when you wash me, it feels really good."

"Marce, maybe we should start bathing separately. I mean, we're almost nine."

"Okay, but let's wait a few weeks. I need to get used to the idea. Hey, maybe Arnie will take baths with me if you're so nervous."

"I am *not* nervous! And mitts off Arnie! I just think it's weird, that's all. My little sisters don't even bathe together anymore. Are you a Pisces or something?"

"India, you *know* I'm a Virgo. I just like the motion of the water when we're both in the tub. It's nothing, really. Besides, I'm developing and you're not. I'm not sure you should be seeing me nude at this point."

Low blow, but I'd rejected her and she was feeling huffy. I wonder if I'd feel tingly if I took a bath with Arnie. Boys have *got* to be easier to deal with. If not, I'm joining a convent. Celesta from across the street says her parents will die if she doesn't become a Sister of the Whispering Vespers. She says she'll die if she does. They're not even allowed to talk! They have to write notes and whistle like pet owners. Oh well. I'm too young to make these decisions. Let's get through third grade and then we'll talk. I might ask Arnie over for a bath anyway, just to be empirical. I

4/30/59

Dear Hope,

I now have my answer to the tingling question.

"Hey, Arn, thanks for coming over."

"No problem. In the shrink biz, we're totally empirical. You mentioned something about testing the bath water for excess chlorine?"

"Well, I sort of lied about that part."

"Whaddya mean? What are we doing?"

"Don't worry, it's still a bath experiment. By the way, Marci hasn't called you this week, has she?"

"Nope."

"Good, I got to you first."

"Huh?"

"Never mind. Did you see that movie with Vincent Price called 'The Tingler'?"

"Yeah..."

"Well, we're gonna re-create it right here in this tub."

"Are you nuts? Why would we do that?"

"Because it would be fun, that's why."

Fun? That thing kills people!"

"Keep your shirt on. We'll just pretend to re-create it. On second thought, take your shirt off. In fact, take all your clothes off."

"*You wanna take a bath together naked?*"

"What, are you shy?"

"Not at all. I have a very nice physique. It's just...aren't we a bit old for this kind of thing?"

"Yes. Now strip. Do it for science!"

Arnie stripped to the bone and we climbed into the tub. He does have a nice physique. I wonder what our kids will look like. I hope they have red hair.

"Ah, the water is just right, Ind. I've been so stressed lately."

"Why? You're just a kid, Arnie."

"I know, but there's lots of tsouris at home. My parents fight a lot, and I have to be the peacemaker."

"Gee, that sucks. Lay back and let me wash you."

"*Wash me?*"

"Yeah. What's wrong with that?"

"India, you know I'm good-natured, but I have boundaries. I'm not letting any girl wash me."

"Okay then, wash me. It's important! I have to find something out. Go ahead, wash."

Arnie scrubbed my skin with a bright yellow washcloth, and sure as pie, I began to tingle.

"Okay, that's enough. I found out all I need to know."

"But what about the Tingler? We have to keep rubbing 'til we see it. Besides. I'm beginning to enjoy this."

"Forget it. My mom's due home any minute."

Arnie was out of the tub and dressed in a flash.

"If there are no other experiments you need me for, I'll be going."

"Actually, there is one more. Have you ever kissed a girl?"

"See ya."

Oh well, you can't blame a girl for trying. I think I'll go to the corner for a hero. I need some oral gratification. Maybe someday Arnie will kiss me and then I won't need carbs. Love, me

CAMPING OUT

7/5/59

Dear Mom,

Camp Natas is okay. We sleep in tents and weave baskets. They call it occupational therapy. My counselor, Dolly, is from the Fillipeens and she talks funny. Yesterday, she told us, "Put your shits away, fucks." Sorry, I was paraphrasing.

My favorite tent mate is Janie, and we're best friends. I get the feeling her parents are loaded because she always mentions someone named Cook. We even barfed at the same time when the camp had a flu outbreak.

The boys here are stupid. The other night we returned from a sing-along and all our panties were gone. We got them back the next day, but the crotches were missing. It feels kind of windy without them.

Three nights ago Dolly woke us in the dead of night and took us to this big, round pit where everyone from the whole camp was sitting. She told us this was the Annual Night of Worship, a camp tradition. The counselors started chanting and doing this weird dance and calling out to someone called Satan (which is, come to think of it, the name of our camp spelled backwards.) Maybe he owns the place. After the fireworks, we finished our Satan burgers and went back to sleep. In the morning, Dolly told us we'd been dreaming. But if that's true, how did we all have the same dream? This place is creepy!

The food isn't so hot, either. They serve rhubarb, which is stringy and sour. Maybe this guy Satan put it on the menu as a joke. Last week there was one day when they only served rice so we could identify with the starving children in India. Well, I'm India and I'm starving! I detest rice. I mean, would it have killed them to add a little cumin? Later, I overheard the camp director telling someone the real reason they have rice day is to save money. Please send spices! Oops, five minutes 'til lights out.

Mommy, I'm sad and scared. I miss you and Emma and Tess so much. I'm not sure I can tolerate it here for two months. Please let me come home. I promise I'll stay in my room and I won't be a problem like I usually am. Pleeaaaasseee!!! I

7/18/59

Dear India,
Sorry for not writing sooner, but I've been in the Greek Isles. I figured since you girls are at camp, I may as well enjoy my freedom. I'm glad you're enjoying yourself, hon. Your sisters write that their camp is fun, too. Sorry about Rice Day. I'll write and ask for a refund. Your father didn't pay three grand so you could starve.

I had a great time in Greece, and I met a handsome doctor on the cruise. He lives in the city and wants to see me this weekend if he has no emergency face lifts. The city is hot and muggy. You're better off in Lake Placid where it's cool. My job is a grind. Lots of briefs to write, and I end up working weekends a lot. I'm sorry the nights are scary, but you'll be home in a few weeks. Stick it out and you'll feel better about yourself. There's nothing for you here. Chin up. And remember, crying is not an option. Love, Mom

7/18/59

Dear Daddy,
How are you? I am fine. No, I'm not. I want to come home! Mom says she's too busy, but the truth is, she doesn't want me around. Daddy, how come I'm always being sent somewhere? Can't I stay at home where I belong? Please call Mommy and ask her—no, beg her—to let me come home. Love, I

7/20/59

Dearest Dear,
By the time you read this you'll almost be home! I called your mom and told her what you said, but she insists she's too busy to look after you. Then she hung up on me. Please call when you get home. We'll have sushi and see a French film. I know how you adore Deneuve. Love, Dad

8/25/59

Dear Hope,
I returned from camp to find Mom's boyfriend, Sam, living with us. No wonder she was so busy this summer. Sam's okay—tall, dark and Jewish—and spends his free time reading articles about mating. I could see it if he were a gyno, but since he's a plastics guy, it seems creepy. If I were well-adjusted, I might actually like Sam. He's a face guy, after all, and my nose could use some improvement down the line. But I resent him cuz Mom loves him more that she loves me and my sisters. I might have to cause trouble over this, despite my deviated septum. Maybe I'll have her paged repeatedly at Bloomingdale's. 'Attention shoppers, please claim your child in ladie's lingerie.' She'll hate that, but I don't care. I need affection! I want Mommy to want me, not some stupid plastic surgeon—although she's not getting any younger and I can certainly see the attraction. Love, Me

9/10/59

Dear Arnie,

I can't believe you're away again! What is a pilgrimage to Mecca, anyway? We studied the Pilgrims in third grade, but I don't remember a place called Mecca. Is it on the west coast?

Yesterday, Sam caught me and Tessa smoking in the shower. He said it's understandable that *I* would indulge in this sort of behavior, but to involve my seven-year-old sister was unforgivable, and he was gonna have to penalize me. Jeez, I know he's upset, but does he have to bring his dick into it? Last year some drunk whipped his thing out in the foyer and I nearly fainted! Yuck, penises are ugly! (Except for yours, of course.) Guess I'd better give up the ciggies 'til the smoke clears. Love, I

7/8/60

Dear Hope,

Well, I'm back at camp, but at least the food is edible at this one. Why does it seem like I'm never home? I'm getting a fucking complex. Ooh, I'd better not say that. If I become famous one day, these diaries might be published and I wouldn't want my readers to think I knew the f-word at such a tender age. Oh, what the fuck. Fuck me! Fuck Mom! Fuck Sam! There, I've sullied myself for posterity. Fuck it. I

10/10/60

Dear Hope,

I've actually been home for three months in a row. Is there a skew here somewhere? And Sam has moved out. Yay! It's no fun living in a psych ward. Mom blames me, of course. *Do you have to ruin my life*? she asked. Yes, actually I do, since she's ruined mine. There's a perverse pleasure that comes from getting even, kind of like the sexual release a serial killer gets from murdering his victims. At least, that's what the Enquirer says. I wouldn't call it a happy feeling, but why should today be different? Love, I

SHRINKAGE

2/10/61

Dear God,

Today mom says I have to see a shrink because I'm a troublemaker, and maybe we can find out what my trouble is. I don't want to go! I'm not crazy. I'm not! If I go I won't tell him anything. I'll just sit there and look neurotic—not a stretch. What if someone in school finds out I'm in therapy? No one will talk to me anymore. They hate me already because I lied and said I'm a Jew. I wish I were. I could use a good seder. God, even though I'm an agnostic, please help mom understand me. She doesn't have to pay someone else to. Love, India Jane Kelly

2/15/61

Dear Hope,

I went to see Dr. Mazur today and he asked about my problems. I told him I don't have any, which I don't, except for the fact that mom hates me. During our session the radiator began clanging. When I asked about it, he said something about intercourse. What does sex have to do with radiators? Do people clang when they have sex? Plus, behind Mazur's chair is a big gross greasy spot where he leans his head. I wonder if he uses Brylkreem. If so, he uses more than a dab. He gives me the creeps. I'm not crazy! Sometimes I feel like I'm the only sane person in the world. India

6/25/62

Dear Arnie,

The good news is, I'm not at camp this summer. The bad news is, I've been seeing Mazur twice a week for two months and he hasn't helped me one bit. Not that I need help. He keeps bringing up sex. Today he showed me photos of kids with abnormally large penises and bosoms, and asked for my opinion. He called them enlarged organs. I didn't notice any musical instruments, just lots of freaky-looking kids. I wonder why he's showing me this. Does he think I have sex problems? Now I probably will. What is a sex problem, anyway? Aren't I too young to have one? I never want to mate! Can't we just be friends?

Hope you're enjoying Camp Freud. What exactly do you do there, sit around the campfire profiling each other? Why can't you go to Camp ComeOnIWannaLayYa like everyone else? Love, I

7/24/62

Dear Arnie,

Thanks for telling me that only people over eighteen can have sex problems. This is a huge relief.

Today Mazur was on the phone during our whole session. He's always on the phone with other patients. It seems to me if he's getting paid all this money, he should focus on the person he's shrinking at the time. Plus, all he has to read is Highlights for Children. I prefer the Trib. I'm gonna tell mom I don't want to go anymore. Love, I

8/15/63

Dear Hope,

If my tears are staining this page, I apologize. (Jesus,

I'm apologizing to my journal. Maybe I *do* have issues.) I told Mommy that Mazur isn't doing me any good. I promised to behave if she lets me stop going. An hour later she said I have to go away to school. In Virginia! No please, I can't stand being away from home anymore! I hate the South! I don't know nothin' about birthin' no babies! I'll get home-sick! I'll die! I'll miss my family so much! (I doubt this is true, but it sounds good.) Mom says I'll be living with foster parents named Jack and Edie Harper, and will be attending a small progressive school in Richmond. She claims I'll love the Harpers and won't ever want to come home (she hopes.) Why do I need foster parents when I already have real ones? I can't believe she's sending me away again! I hope I die so I won't have to go. Hope!!!!!!!!!!

ARNIE MAKES HIS MOVE

August 1963

Dear Hope,

I'm walking on air!!!! Arnie proposed today!!!! Here's the lowdown:

"Arn, it's so great to see you! Thanks for inviting me over. I love Stuyvesant Town. It's so Jewish."

"Actually, this is Peter Cooper. Everyone has trouble telling them apart. Cooper's better. Jeez, I can't believe your mom is sending you away to school. How come she keeps sending you places?"

"Simple. She doesn't want me around. She says I drive her crazy. Talk about abandonment issues—I think I'm developing clinical depression!"

"You've always had that", said Arnie, putting his arm around me. "Listen, all kids drive their parents crazy. It's our job. Take my parents, for instance. No, I mean it. Take them!"

"Arnie, you're so funny."

"*Arnie Cohen, get into this kitchen right now! You're lunch is ice cold. Honestly, you drive me crazy. I'm getting a migraine just thinking about it! Oy! Your sister is so well behaved, so good to her mamela. Just wait 'til your father*" *gets home! Oh, here he is now. Julius, your son is giving me such agita! How we ever gave birth to such a putz..."*

"See? All parents hate their kids. What makes yours any different?"

"Oh, Arnie, you're such a comfort. When I talk to Mazur it's just the usual 'New York Superkid from at least one broken home' psycho-babble crap. You're lucky you're not in analysis. It's such bullshit."

Arnie grinned.

"I see a shrink twice a week."

"You do????"

"Sure! If I'm gonna be one, I need to get my own head shrunk. And I'm not the only one in class who goes, either. Marcy does, and Jessica, and Neddie, too."

"Neddie Greenberg sees a shrink? Jeez, his parents must be really disappointed. Just last week he stuck dog shit in Stuie's shoe. Does your shrink relate everything to sex?"

"Nah, you've got a Freudian. They're the worst. Everything is symbolic and fraught with guilt and repressed sexuality. It's not healthy for kids. I think it fucks you up, and then it helps because you're fucked up, whereas if you hadn't gone into analysis, you wouldn't be fucked up in the first place."

"My sentiments exactly. Mazur keeps asking what my problems are. I didn't have any when I got there, except for the fact that I come from a totally dysfunctional family, and have the feeling I'm adopted. Other than that I was fine. Now that I've been seeing him for three months, I've got mucho problemos, mostly centering on the fact that I've been seeing him for three months. Tell me, what does a noisy radiator have to do with sex?"

"Well, I'm only up to Psych 101, but I'd say that because radiators are warm and steamy, and sex is warm and steamy, there might be a connection."

"Oh, give me a break!"

"Okay, how about this? Radiators make noise, and sex is

noisy, so maybe—"

"Forget it, Arn. There's no connection. By the way, how do you know so much about sex?"

"I found my parents' sex manual. Did you know if you touch yourself in— "

"Shut up. I'm too young to know."

"Did you ask your shrink what the radiator-sex connection was?"

Yes. He asked what I thought it was. Why do shrinks do that? Jesus, you'd think that for a buck a minute they'd try to be a bit more accommodating. Will you be like that, Arn?"

"Nah. By the time I'm a shrink, I'll charge a hundred an hour and prescribe drugs. I believe in empathy. And I definitely won't be a Freudian. Plus, none of that role reversal shit where you talk to an empty chair and pretend it's your mother. I don't need a chair to talk to my mom—"

"*Arnie, so help me, get your tuchus into this kitchen. Julius, carry your pipsqueak son to this table! How good a head doctor will he be if he doesn't get decent nourishment? Julius? Hey, wake up! Your tie is in the soup!*"

"—and she definitely doesn't need a chair to talk to me. In fact, she doesn't even need *me* to talk to me. Once I went out for a Good Humor, and when I got back she was still yapping. Didn't even know I'd left. My poor father."

"Yeah, but at least your folks are still together. It's so cozy here. You have a family, you're well adjusted, and your mom makes kugel. May I move in?"

"Actually, I've been meaning to talk to you about that."

"Really?"

"Yes. India, will you marry me?"

"*Marry you?*"

"Yes. I've wanted to ask since we were kids."

"But we still *are* kids. Chronologically, at least. Mentally we're quite mature. My last achievement test put me at college level. And self-parenting takes its toll. In fact, I found my first gray hair yesterday, and—"

"India, I just proposed. What do you say?"

"Arnie, we can't get married now, we're only twelve. I know we've bathed together and stuff, but marriage is more complex. Besides, I'm not having sex 'til I'm married. Oh, but I guess we *would* be married, wouldn't we? Heh heh. Still, I don't feel ready for marriage. I mean, we've never even dated. Gee, isn't this a bit sudden? I think I'm having an anxiety attack. I seem to be having trouble breathing—"

"Relax. I didn't mean *now*. I meant when we're older, after college."

"Oh phew! I feel better already! Sure Arn, it would be an honor being your wife. India Cohen. Just think. I'll finally be a Jew. Well, I'll sound like one, anyway. Do you think your mom would teach me to make kreplachs?"

"Only if you kiss me."

"Gee, I don't know. I've never kissed anyone before and—hey! Um, that wasn't so bad. Oh hi, Mrs. C!"

Hope, I think all moms having homing devices in their vaginas, because they always seem to know when you're thinking of doing stuff with yours.

"Hey, what are you kids up to?"

"Nothing, Mom. India has a sore throat and I was checking for staph."

"With your tongue?"

"Sure. I'm preparing for a career in medicine, if you remember."

"Yeah, I know. And in a few years you'll be using the same excuse when I walk in on something else! *I'm performing a pelvic, be right out!*" You men are all alike! I suppose you'll fall asleep at the table just like your father."

I smiled winningly at Mrs. C.

"It was lovely seeing you again. Mom."

Mrs. C cut her eyes.

"Arnie, what did she mean by that?"

"Arnie's asked me to marry him. Isn't that wonderful?"

"Marry? Oy, my god! Twelve years old and he's already tying himself down. And to a Gentile, no less! Well, I forbid it! Julius, wakey wakey. I need a Milltown!"

I grinned. "God, I just adore your family, Arn. I feel so comfy with all the yelling. It's just like home. Bye, lovey. I'll miss you."

As I walked toward the elevator, it sounded like Arnie and his mom were finally bonding.

" *Mom, relax. Sit in your favorite chair and breathe. Okay, see this other chair? Let's pretend your father is sitting there. Go ahead and tell him how much you despise men and that it's all his fault. Come on, Mom. Let it all out!!*"

"*Julius! Help me! Julie, please—*"

And so, dear Hope, my future is secure. Charlie Brown said the secret of happiness is having three things to look forward to and none to dread. This is one. I only need two more. I'd look forward to getting old, but I know myself too well. But if I can't look forward to old age, what else is there? Death? I don't see this as a viable alternative. I'm damned either way. Senility seems cool. That way you can be old and young at once. Love, *India Kelly Cohen*

VIRGINIA REAL

10/3/63

Dear Arnie,

I've been living with my foster parents, Edie and Jack, for a month now. You might be asking yourself why I need foster parents when I already have two regular ones, but you won't get an answer from me. Jack is working on a new invention—a tiny machine that moves words around. It's no bigger than a TV and you can erase all your mistakes and start over. (Wish I could.) Edie spends every non-working moment in front of the tube. Sometimes she smokes this weird-smelling shit and then she's in a good mood for the rest of the evening. She blew some in my face once, and I laughed a lot at Red Skelton afterward.

Free To Be Me sucks. They call it a Progressive school, and there are only forty students. They put me in the sixth form with the seniors because I have a 165 IQ, but I'm having trouble keeping up. I don't know what I want to be when I grow up, but it sure as shit won't involve physics, calculus or plankton. Why can't I be back at Village Friends with you? I miss Jews. I miss kugel. I miss you. I

10/10/63

Dear Arn,

Thanks for the warm birthday wishes and the psych

textbook. I'll try harder to make friends with my id, but it's my ego that's bugging me these days. I can't believe I'm finally a teenager! I sure don't look like one. I'm still a Carpenter's Dream and I don't have my period. Plus, I'm getting really tired of stuffing my bra, and Edie is getting suspicious at the Kleenex turnover. I dyed my hair red today to celebrate my entry into the teen years, and now I look like Danny Kaye. I wish I were Chinese. They have great hair, though I'd miss my peripheral vision.

Jack has been giving me these massages in the morning to wake me up. I asked for an alarm, but Jack says he prefers the human touch. He rubs me all over, and it's quite relaxing, but some of the places he touches are places I've never been touched before. Oh well, I guess it's not hurting anyone, and at least I'm not tingling. I

11/22/63

A: JFK is dead. There's nothing on TV. I

1/11/64

Dear Arnie,

It was great seeing you over Christmas—or in your case, Hanukkah. By the way, what do gefilte fish look like when they're alive? Do they eat plankton? I have three quarts in my locker and it's not getting any fresher.

That joke you told about foreskin wallets still has me chuckling. You rub them and they turn into suitcases! Ha! I still cannot believe your parents bronzed yours. Maybe it will be worth something later on when they rub it! Ha!

Well, back to the salt mines. The river is frozen over, thank god, so no more plankton retrievals for a while. Maybe I'll abuse myself 'til spring. I have a ready supply of blades from Jack's razor. Love, I

WENDY VEGA

5/2/64

Dear Arn,

Thanks for your concern about Jack's Russian hands and Roman fingers. No, I've never seen his thing! Why do you ask? I wouldn't mind seeing yours again, now that we're older. It was pretty small when we were eight.

I love spring in Richmond. I've been listening to the radio Jack bought me for being a 'willing subject', as he calls me. I adore Peter and Gordon, and Bob Dylan, who can't sing worth shit but says lots of heavy things. I detest the Beatles, however. They're too commercial and the sound won't last. Lennon is cute, but if I saw him, I wouldn't scream. Maybe I'm jaded. Can one be jaded at thirteen? I feel like my mind is being sanded down like an old wood floor. Let me escape this prison that is youth! (Fuck George Bernard Shaw.) I

7/16/64

Dear Arn,

It's summer and my sisters are away at camp. I was too, but I got kicked out for dying my hair black. (I guess my hairdresser isn't the only one that knows for sure.) I'm alone with mom and I hate her, so I'm becoming rebellious. Please come home soon, and don't forget to kiss the Wailing Wall for me. Or is the Blarney Stone? Either way, wipe your mouth after. Not everyone is as hygienic as we are. Love, I

8/24/64

Arn,

It's been a long, hot summer. On the one hand, I know Mom doesn't want me around, but on the other, I'm left blissfully alone each weekend while she visits her columnist (and Communist) boy friend in DC. How ironic, that when I'm down south she's up here, and when I'm here, she's there.

Sometimes my friends sleep over, but usually I'm by myself smoking, Mom's Tarrytons (no inhaling), and entering Murray The K's call-in contests. Last week I won a Jose Jimenez album. I often take advantage of my glorious time alone by dressing up in Mom's evening clothes and walking around the Village barefoot. Tonight I dropped a Papaya Dog on her silk cocktail dress. Hee hee. I'm having a ball! I just wish someone would come home soon, as I'm feeling kind of lonely. I

9/25/64

Arn,

It's still warm in Richmond, but I no longer belong here. I've changed. I feel like I'm being shoved into a shoe that is sizes too small. I must call Dr. Mazur and see if he can get me out of here. I've had so many massages I could teach classes! I

9/28/64

Arn,

Update!!! Mazur tried, but it seems Mother is determined to keep me in Richmond 'til I die or finish high school, whichever comes first. It's gonna be a horse race. I

11/20/64

Dear Arn,

Remember when I came home in October to find Mom had given my room to Emma? I still feel neurotic and upset by it. She's dumped me in a closet, really—definitely not a room for someone who's around much. I can't believe she gave away my room! Does Freud have a chapter on this? I didn't ask to be sent away, and now she's taken the one thing that was truly mine and I hate her! I hate my life! I hate my sisters! Why aren't they away at school, too? Because they're ass-kissers, that's why. But they'll get theirs soon.

I have big plans for them during Christmas break involving Librium and gaffer's tape.

Jack is touching me more lately. I'm afraid to tell, cuz Jack said he'd kill me if I do. He likes that I'm finally developing, and says he hopes one day to 'give me real pleasure'. Truthfully, I'd prefer dark chocolate. I need help, Arn. I need some coping tools. Also, could you send some Dubble Bubble? They don't have it down here. I

12/30/64

Dear Arn,

Late last night Edie and Jack had a huge fight. She was screaming that I have to go because I'm too grown up to live here now. (I *have* gone down to one Kleenex per cup, but I didn't realize Edie was monitoring so carefully). I called Mom in hysterics this morning, but she won't budge. Would your folks consider adopting me? I could work, and I don't eat that much. Okay, that's a lie. I *do* eat that much. Plus, then you'd be my brother and we couldn't get married. On to Plan B—for Breakdown.

By the way, I know I alarmed you with my Christmas plans for Emma and Tess, but what I meant was, *I'd* take the Librium. As for the tape, I'll leave that to your imagination. Love, I

1/22/65

Dear Arn,

Update!!! I'm getting out of here! I finally spilled the beans to Mazur about the massages, and I'm on the next bus home! Mom has enrolled me at James T. Kirk High to save money, but I don't care. Anything to get away from Jack. You'll have to massage me once in awhile though, to keep my endorphins in shape. Sayonara, Richmond!!!!! I

THE LOW DOWN
ON HIGH SCHOOL

2/1/65

Dear Arn,

I can't believe now that I'm back in the city, your parents have sent you to live on a kibbutz! Wasn't a bar mitzvah enough? Do you have to live among your people to prove you're a good Jew? (Is there room for me?)

Mom enrolled me in Kirk High, and it isn't pretty. This sure isn't the elite Village crowd we grew up with. And everyone has already formed cliques. Maybe I'll drop out and model after I get that growth spurt the doctor promised. L'chaim. I

2/15/65

Dear Arnie,

So how's Israel? Can you speak Yiddish yet? It's cool that you pick grapefruits and eat kugel, but psychoanalyzing the locals for sheckels sounds a bit premature. You have a long way to go before you become a shrink, and you don't want to inadvertently bring Dr. Mengele to mind.

In your absence I've made a new best friend. Her name is Lydia Sarkesian and she's Armenian. She has olive skin and tons of curly brown hair, but her nose isn't the smallest. In short, she looks like one of your people. We met in Algebra class. I mentioned that I had attended a progressive school called Free To Be Me, but that I left because I wasn't.

"Wasn't what, India?"

"Free to be me. Hey Lydia, it's so nice to finally have a friend here. Can you speak Double G? Madagy nadagame is India."

"Eww, it sounds like gagging."

"Kind of. It's one of those stupid languages kids speak thinking no one will understand them, like Pig Latin. Hadagow adagare yadagou? What did I say?"

"Beats me. Sounds Pakastanian."

"I asked how you are."

"I get it! It's like the way Murray the K used to talk. Meeazurry the Keeeazay and all that, right?"

"Exactly! Lydia, you and I understand each other perfectly, even if we don't speak the same language."

We grinned at each other, knowing a long and fulfilling friendship lay ahead.

So, Arn, how's your buddy, Elon? He kissed me over the holidays but I haven't heard from him since. He's a really sloppy kisser. If we make out again I'm definitely taking Contac. Isn't that supposed to dry you up? Love, I

2/24/65

Dear Arn,

Elon says *I'm* a sloppy kisser? Jeez, I had to swab the floor after he left, the fuckhead!

Remember I told you about Lydia? Today during roll call she taught me the meaning of life.

"Olga Dubcek?"

"Here."

"India Kelly?"

"Here."

"Lydia Sarkesian?"

"Here. And Mrs. Gewirtz, may I say how nice it is to have you as a teacher? I've learned so much from you already."

Glancing around for Allen Funt, Mrs. G began writing equations on the board.

"Jesus, Lyd," I whispered. "You sound like Eddie Haskell's younger sister, you brownnosing little shit. What gives?"

Lydia raised her notebook to her face, whereupon she whispered the Golden Rule of Brownnosing.

"India, you have to learn to play the game. If you don't, they'll eat you alive."

"Who?"

"Who what?"

"Who's gonna eat me alive?"

"*They*, India! The people who run things. The Great Unwashed. Whoever. Don't say I didn't warn you."

I don't know, Arn. Maybe I need help in this area. I'm not exactly a fucking diplomat. But I hate people. How can you be nice to people when you detest their very existence? Anyway, after Algebra, Lyd walked me up the Down staircase to our next class.

"Ind, I love your outfit. I wish I had the nerve to dress like that."

"Like what?"

"You know, green fishnets, black stilettos, the green streak in your hair—"

"Well, you can't say I'm not coordinated."

"You're very trendy. Maybe you'll start a new fad. My dad says fads are the work of the devil. Or is it fags? Whatever. He thinks everything is the work of the devil, even my mom, because she withholds sex. She claims they've done it five times, once for each of us. Strange, to think we're products of our fathers' orgasms. I'm never fucking. In fact, I'm thinking of becoming a nun."

"Since when? Lydia, how could you? You'd miss so much of life! Besides, God can't be brownnosed, so don't even bother."

"What else besides sex would I miss?"

"Well, have you been to the top of the Empire State Building? I hear it's far out! And then there's the Statue of Liberty and Ellis Island—"

"India, I can be a nun and still sightsee. I knew it! You can't think of one good reason I shouldn't join the Order of the Murmuring Vespers."

"Murmuring Vespers? It sounds like a subdivision of Forest Lawn. And yes, I *can* give you one very good reason. If you become a nun we can't take drugs and fuck our brains out."

"But Ind, I'm not allowed to do that anyway. I have to be home by eight, even on weekends."

"Don't worry. As soon as we turn eighteen I'll take you away from here."

"Okay, but Poppa will put an Armenian curse on you."

"Ooooh, I'm quaking in my go-go boots."

"And I'll never have green hair."

"Fine, I don't need the competition, anyway. But tomorrow, you're wearing fishnets to school, and I won't take no for an answer."

Arnie, it's so great having a best friend. Never mind that Lydia and I have totally different values. She likes me and that's enough. Wish I did. I need to learn self-adulation, and I think I have the perfect tool. It's called LSD. They're using it at Harvard to attain bliss, though I've heard reports of people jumping out of windows on the stuff. I'll try some and report back soonest, if I haven't defenestrated in the meantime. Love, I

YELLOW FINGERS

5/23/67

Dear Lydia,

I met the most outasite guy at the Psychedelic Panther last night! And to think I nearly didn't go because my purple go-go boots were being resoled! But Betsy Harrod—you know, the chick who wears fishnets in gym?—talked me into going.

"It's full of hot guys from Queens. You'll cream!"

"But Betsy, my boots—"

"Relax, you can wear mine. India, you *need* this. Tell you what. If you go I'll lend you my Yardley Slickers lipstick in 'Corpse-like Silver'. It's their newest shade."

"You've got Corpse-like Silver? Shrimpton hasn't even modeled that yet. Okay, I'm in!"

Lyd, the Panther is teeny-bopper heaven. You have to be eighteen to get in, but Patsy procured a baptismal certificate declaring me to be Theresa Bongiorno, nee 1947, so, no problem. The walls are plastered with day-glo posters, pulsating under black lights. The dance floor is a wall-to-wall carpet of undulating hippies. I'd been there two minutes when I knew Betsy was right. I *did* need this. The Village is funereal compared to this. In that first moment inside, I was emboldened with the blood of freedom. It was then that I claimed adulthood as mine, and knew I'd never be lonely again.

"Anyone got a ciggie?" I asked brazenly, like the hussy I was fast becoming.

"India, you don't smoke!"

"I do now!"

Betsy led me to a table where a group of guys was ogling a short black chick doing the Panther Shuffle. Her name was Lola, and she was definitely shaking her money-maker. A short Puerto Rican called Pee Wee shoved a pack of Marlboros in my face and asked if I wanted to ball.

"Base or foot?"

Betsy explained that balling was another name for fucking, and I told Pee Wee I'd get back to him. Pee Wee's cousin Azteca stopped ogling Lola long enough to hand me his lighter, but when I saw Betsy's hand on his dick, I lit my own. It was then that I came face to face with Adonis—aka Tony Messina. Oh god, oh rapture, oh... shit! Alas, at that very second, I inhaled my first puff of tar and nicotine *ever* and keeled over. Fortunately, Tony was there to catch me as I swooned. While I lay there staring into his sapphire eyes, I re-swooned several times, and was momentarily distracted by the possibility that I might be coming in front of strangers, but since nothing was tingling I decided I was just happy.

"You must be India", crooned Tony. " I've heard about you."

"Nothing too incriminating, I hope", I warbled. " No matter what Betsy's told you, I *do* have sexual feelings. I'm a bit self-involved, I admit, but it's due to fear of rejection. See, it all began—"

"India, you don't have to explain yourself. I'm sure you're a beautiful person. By the way, I'm Tony Messina. Wanna do the Jerk?"

"Is that like balling?" I asked skeptically.

"Nah, it's just a dance."

"Whew! Okay, sure, why not?"

— 30 —

"Hey, you wanna black beauty to take the edge off?"

I considered the question.

"Jeez, I know blacks have great rhythm, but I'd rather dance with you."

"India, a black beauty is an upper. It makes you feel like you're on top of the world!" He reached into the pocket of his chartreuse crushed velvet jeans. "Here, I have an extra."

"Okay, sure. Whatever."

What the fuck, right, Lyd? Speaking of fucking, how can guys ask you to fuck them—excuse me, *ball* them—when they've known you for ten seconds? Isn't there some sort of incubation period or something?

While I waited for the speed to come on, Tony and I swayed to the sound of Otis Redding bemoaning the black unemployment rate. Though I'm not overly sympathetic to anyone who sits around on a dock instead of working, it's a pretty song and I was starting to feel really nice. I continued feeling great for the rest of the night, during which time I smoked three packs of Marlboros, and my white Yardley nail polish turned canary yellow. Not to mention my lungs, I'm sure. I was flying, Lyd! I was telling anybody anything. My lips kept moving, no longer under my control. Yap, yap, puff, puff. Tony watched the monster he had created, and grinned. And the beat went on.

"Hey Tony, do you have an old lady? No? Jeez, you're such a fox. Oh, you recently broke up? I'm so sorry! (Hah!) Me? Yeah, I was seeing this guy Kenny but he wanted me to touch his dick so I split. Why buy the cow, and all that bullshit. Boy, these ups are far out! Is it hot in here to you? Hey, remember when Lucy did that Vitameatavegamin ad and after a few swigs asked if anyone else felt warm? Jesus, I wonder if there were ups in that stuff. I love Lucy, don't you? What a great name for a show. By the way, did you see *Bewitched* last night? Samantha is finally wearing a mini! My mom just started wearing one, too. She even smokes a joint sometimes when she wins a case. She asked me to smoke with her once, but that's like watching your parents fuck. I think forty is too old to be acting hip. Even thirty is pushing it. I'll never wear a mini after thirty. The Flying Nun doesn't wear one, though I'm sure Sally Field does—"

On and on I rapped, loving the sound of my own voice, trying to keep my head on. Tony finally shut me up by ramming against me for a good night kiss. He promised to call later, and Betsy and I cabbed it back to the Village. At four AM I felt like I'd had the best night of my life. By five, I felt like dying and grew concerned.

"Betsy, I feel like shit. Could I have picked up any diseases at the Panther?"

"Ind, you're not sick, you're crashing."

"But we're not in a car."

"From the pills! When you take ups, the better you feel now, the worse you'll feel later. Unless you take a down. Personally, I prefer them. You get horny, you fuck whoever's around, and then you pass out. Of course acid is groovy too. One time I—"

"Bets, I love you, but spare me the fish stories. There's nothing more boring that hearing about someone else's trips. I'm calling Daddy."

"Why are you calling *him*?"

"He's in the drug business. He'll know what to do."

"India, he writes ads for Pepto Bismol, he's not a pharmacist. Besides, it's five AM."

"That's OK. Ever since D-Day he sleeps with one eye open. Hello, Daddy? Oh, sorry. I know it's early, but I took these black pills someone slipped into my Pepsi and—who was it? Betsy—yeah, little Betsy. You'd never know to look at her. 'Kay, I promise. Bye."

"What did he say?"

"He says to take two aspirin and that he forgives you for drugging me."

"*Me?* It was Tony! Now I'll be blamed for something I didn't even do! No good deed goes unpunished."

"Which good deed was that?"

"Oh, never mind."

"Patsy, bliss out. Daddy was half asleep. He won't remember a thing in the morning. "

"It *is* morning! Let's try to sleep."

"Gosh, I don't think I can stop rapping long enough to sleep."

"Shit, here's a Seconal. You'll sleep for a friggin' week."

"Thanks, Bets. You're the greatest. "

"You're welcome. Tomorrow we'll do some killer windowpane. It's cut with baby laxative that makes you shit like a bird, but enhances the hallucinations."

"Cool, but let's not do any more *real* drugs. I promised Daddy."

So Lyd, I'm sitting by the phone waiting for Tony's call. Please come home soon. Do they have good hash in Armenia? Is that the place where they cut your hand off for stealing? What do they cut off if you commit adultery? On second thought, don't tell me. Love, I

5/24/67

Dear Arnie,

I met this great guy named Tony last night. I'll never stop wanting you, but I'm lonely and you're always away. I hope Tony calls soon because I'm obsessing about him nonstop. Love is such as trip, Arn. You're in hell one minute, heaven the next. It's like an E Ticket ride at Disneyland only you don't throw up—unless you do peyote. Let me know soonest if you've had any, ahem, experiences. I haven't yet, but I'm a month older than you, so I probably will in the near future. Have fun at the kibbutz and don't kiss anyone named Rachel. I'll know, Love, I

PISS ALLEY

7/10/67

Dear Lyd,

I'm so happy you're moving home soon because your mom is homesick for the projects. That being the case, I'd hate to spend an extended period of time in Armenia. I finally had my first date with Tony last weekend! After spending the evening at Figaro's, we walked over to Piss Alley in the East Village, the hip place to take a leak after a night of boozing, etc. (Lennon pissed there last year, which may explain its legendary status.)

Tony is gorgeous. I can't believe he asked me, out of all the chicks at the Panther, to be his old lady. I just hope he doesn't expect me to ball him. I didn't tell you before, because your letters were being censored, but Kenny from the Wha tried to make me touch his dick in May, and I freaked. He called me a prude, but I'm not a prude, Lyd. I just believe in waiting for marriage to touch a guy's dick.

Anyways, Tony and I rapped on the way to Piss Alley.

"Hey, Tony, how come you're attracted to me? I'm skinnier than Twiggy and flatter, too. Plus, I'm still a virgin and plan to remain one."

"Bullshit. It's the Summer of Love. You'll lose it before the year is out. Besides, my schwanz is eight inches. You've gotta see it!"

I asked Tony to define schwanz, foolishly hoping it was his inseam measurement.

"It's my dick, India. My dick is eight inches!"

Marone! Not that I have a frame of reference, unless you count the tip of Kenny's, or Mr. Dubcek's dildo, but it sounded huge. I'm assuming eight inches is the length and not the width. Jesus, can you imagine? I didn't know whether to run screaming or worship the ground he stood on. When we finally arrived at Piss Alley, Tony tugged at his zipper, and I hid my face.

"Don't be afraid, babe. Here's your chance to see my schwanz! It's now or never."

I voted for never.

"Oh Tony, I'd really rather not. I don't think my heart could take it. I mean, I'm tripping my brains out and I'm sure your, er, schwanz is so overwhelming I'd assume I was hallucinating."

Schwanz rebuffed, Tony went into a corner and pissed for like five hours. Due to the seedy locale, I started having hallucinations featuring the Sharks and the Jets, and was just about to launch into 'Officer Krupke' when Tony beckoned.

"Hey babe, let's make it."

Tony kissed me and ground against me hard. I began feeling bruised, and pulled away. Tony was panting, which I figured was due to dehydration from his recent marathon piss. He's a really good kisser, Lyd, but even at the height of his hard-on, I didn't feel eight inches in either direction. Then he did the unthinkable. He slid into second base.

"Hey, get your hand off my bra! And quit breathing like that! It sounds like you're having a bad trip!"

"Please, India, let me touch your tits. They're so small and firm and—"

"Get away or I'll cry rape!" That always gets 'em.

"Baby, please, I have needs! I have DSB. I'll get blue

balls! I promise you'll still be a technical virgin. Puleeze, I'm begging!"

Just then I spied Pee Wee, Azteca and the rest of the gang. Azteca's radio was blaring some song by Sam and Dave about coming (how apropos), and I extricated my battered body from Tony's. We each saluted the troops, albeit in different ways.

Lola is a trip. In addition to the Panther Shuffle, she's taught me several twelve-letter words, and for this I am eternally grateful. My mom hates Lola, which is reason enough to dig the motherfucker. Pee Wee and Azteca are cousins and best friends. I've made out with both of them, though I have a huge crush on Azteca's brother Chico, because he looks like Lennon. Still, I think I'm in love with Tony. Chico has an old lady, so I'm stuck with Tony anyways. He seems nice, even if he does beg for sex.

After everyone finished pissing, we took the train to Pee Wee's uncle's club in Red Hook. (They call it a pool hall, but I think it's one of those places where the Mafia hangs out and orders hits.) We spent the balance of the night sacked out at the Ortiz Pool Emporium. Pee Wee tried to stick it to Lola, who was sacked out on the pool table, but she cried rape and he backed off. By morning I was firmly entrenched as Tony's old lady. So how come I still feel lonely?

How is the Summer of Love playing out in Armenia? I heard about the rioting over there, for the right to wear bells. Are you guys that desperate for entertainment? Miss you terribly. I

SEX, LIES AND AFTERGLOW

6/28/68

Dear Arnie,

Free at last! School is out and so am I. Wish you were here.

Check this out. Last week I'm strutting down MacDougal wearing the Charles Jourdan pumps I bought with my measly graduation check. My mini was just below my ass and my legs were tanned. I looked hot. I don't mean to imply that I was happy, because I wasn't. I was as miserable as ever. I'm okay when I have a boyfriend, but usually I'm dysphoric most of the time, as you know.

So there I was, outside the Waverly Theatre, scouring the Village for the man of my nightmares. I'm not picky. The first guy that passed wore a wedding ring, but I'm not that desperate. Yet. A few minutes later this great-looking guy approached. As he drew closer, I noticed his hair was really long and he had huge breasts, and soon realized it was my friend Laura from Canarsie. I vowed to see an optometrist posthaste.

"Laura, how's it hanging?" I asked.

"Okay, but Dave kicked me out and I have no place to crash. Can I stay witchu, Ind?"

"Gee, I'm not sure. Mom hates bridge-and-tunnel people. She has problems with their grammar."

"Whaddya mean? I speak perfect English. Da rain in Spain fawls mainly on da plain. See? She'll love me, I sweah!"

"Okay, but let's find some guys, I'm horny as shit. Jesus and I didn't work out, and he has a new old lady. She's thirty. How can he go down on someone that old?"

"I dunno, Ind. Maybe he puts a bag ovah her head and plays a BeeGees rekid so he can't hear her moan."

"Hey, how did you know Jesus puts on the Bee Gees when he fucks?"

"Uh—you tol' me?"

"Shit, you fucked Jesus! Christ, how could you do this to me? I thought we were friends."

"India, you blasphemed one too many times in dat sentence. So I fucked him. Big deal! It was ages ago, before you knew him. God, I'm so psyched about livin' wit you! You can iron my hair and I'll teach you how to give blow jobs."

"Laura, I didn't say you could live with me. I said you could crash for a few days."

"Oh, sure, I unnerstand. Your mom won't even know I'm around. She's gone most of the time anyways, ain't she? Don't she travel all ova wit her Commie boyfriend?"

"He's not a Communist, he's a *columnist* for the Washington Times, and one of Nixon's best friends."

"Jeez, dat's worse than bein' a Commie! How come your mom digs him? She's so left-winged."

"I dunno. I think she's impressed by him. She defended him once when he refused to reveal his sources. Seems he got some inside dope from a guy called Deep Shit or something, but he wouldn't reveal the guy's name."

"Deep shit?"

"Yeah, he's some small-time snitch in DC. Paul—that's my mom's boyfriend—says the guy isn't reliable and no one will use him again cuz his credibility is shot. Here we are at

Washington Square. I'm gonna pick up the first guy I see. Hey, there's a cute one. Excuse me sir, may I speak with you for a moment?"

"Sure, my name's Mike. What's your sign?"

"Open for business. I'm India and this is Laura. We're both Libras."

"India, that's a groovy name. Wanna come back to my place and fuck? You're both welcome."

Mike's wavy hair and blue saucer eyes were so hypnotic, I could nearly overlook the acnes pustules that covered his face and neck.

"Okay, but I hope it's air-conditioned. It must be a hundred degrees out."

"Sure. I live on 5th between B and C, and there are lots of bullet holes in the walls which create cross ventilation."

"Oh well, I guess that's okay. You coming, Laura?"

"Nah, I'm going ova Dave's. Maybe if I fuck him he'll give me somma dat killer Windowpane and I'll share it witchu later."

Mike and I walked over to Alphabet City and into Mike's pad, which smelled like Raid. He gestured proudly.

"Isn't it outasite?"

I looked around cautiously. "It's groovy. Would you mind sweeping the roaches off that glass so I can have some water?"

"No prob. Look, they're all rushing back under the fridge where they belong. Want some Purple Haze?"

"Sure. I love acid."

"Groovy! It's a dynamite aphrodisiac. You'll be creaming in your jeans before you know it. Come on, let's fuck."

"Wait! I'm not peaking yet. How about turning on some vibes to get us in the mood?"

"Okay, I'll put on the new Beatles album. C'mon!"

Mike was the proud owner of a Murphy bed, which he pulled off the wall with a flourish, dislodging a water bug the size of Gregor Samsa. Though I'd rather sleep in the subway tracks than within a hundred feet of a roach, the acid was kicking in. As I undressed, I flashed on Laura's run-in with a water bug a week earlier. As she tells it, she put on her shower cap and a humongous roach crawled out. Naked and screaming, she ran into the hall where the Italian ladies thought she was being raped. The police were called. They weren't thrilled to be summoned away from the donut shop for a stupid bug, but they shot it anyway. Laura fellated them both out of gratitude.

"India, you smell so great. What are you wearing?"

"Evening in Canarsie. Ooooh, that feels good, Mike. What are you doing?"

"Taking my boots off. Boy, this shit is better than I thought."

"Oooh, that's nice, too. Wait! I don't have my diaphragm in yet!"

"Don't worry, you won't need it with me."

"Why? Are you shooting blanks?"

"*Are you kidding*?? I'm Italian! Shooting blanks—that'll be the day."

"Then why don't I need my diaphragm?"

"Because when it hotter outside than in, you can't get pregnant."

"Oh, come on! Do you expect me to believe that shit?"

"I swear on my mother's grave. If it's hotter outside than body temperature, the sperm fall asleep."

"Well, if you're sure—"

After we'd finished, Mike seemed impressed.

"India, you were great! Where did you learn those moves?"

"Earlier this year I dated Jesus."

"Oh, that explains it. Let's get some sleep."

It was three AM, but when I began hallucinating pork lo mein, I knew I had to eat. I was just about to call for take-out when I heard something troubling.

"Hey, Mike, what the fuck is going on? Who's yelling?"

"It's one of my roommates, Terry. He always screams after he shoots up. Then he pukes."

I freaked.

"Jeez, turn on the stereo so we don't have to listen. Christ, I'm having a really bad trip now. I hate hearing people puke!"

Mike smiled. "I love it. It's so cleansing. Oh wow, 'Hey Jude' is playing. I love this cut!"

"Me too. I think it's about the holocaust."

Mike smirked. "Personally, I don't think there was a holocaust. I think the Jews were going for the attention. Okay, the puking is over. Now Terry goes into Vince's room. They're lovers."

"Why is Terry wielding a butcher knife? Is it some sort of kinky sex thing?"

"No, He's trying to kill Vince again. I'd better call the cops. Oh shit, Vince *is* a cop! We'd better let them fight it out."

"Are you high?! I'm not gonna stand here and become a murder witness. I'm splitting. This trip has been a total nightmare! Dear God, I swear I'll never pick up a stranger again if you get me outta here. And Mike, fuck you and your soporific sperm!"

I arrived home to find Laura on my stoop.

"Hi Ind. You said I could stay witchu, so I was waitin."

"Jeez, if Terry hadn't tried to kill Vince, I would've been out all night. You're luck there was violence and I came home."

"You're jokin'. Terry tried to kill Vince again? He musta done some killer scag. Was he barfin'?"

"Hey, how do you know about Vince and Terry? We just met Mike this aft—oh jeez, you fucked Mike, too?"

"Yeah, I met him at the Wha last week."

"Laura, is there anyone in the Village you haven't fucked?"

"Yeah, but you don't know him. Let's go to bed."

"Laura, are you stoned? You're weaving."

"Hanh? No, I ain't stoned. I only had twelve black Russians."

"Oh god, you're gang banging Commies now?"

"It's a drink, India."

Oh. Hey, you're not gonna get sick are you? I've heard enough puking for one night."

"Nah, give me some bread and I'll be cool."

"Here, eat the whole loaf. I'm not taking chances."

After ingesting several slices of Arnold Brick Oven, Laura climbed into my twin bed and began to wriggle.

"Will you quit it? I can't sleep!"

"Sorry, Ind. I almost passed out earlier, but now I'm wide awake."

"Oh swell. It's four AM, you're chatty, and I'm crashing from some shitty acid I got for fucking some anti-Semitic asshole. I suppose you wanna rap."

"Yeah. Boy this bed is tiny. How do you sleep in it?"

"It's a twin, Laura. It's made for one person. That's why they call it a twin."

"Wouldn't a twin be for two people? Why don't they call it a single?"

"I don't know. Let's call Messrs. Sealy and Posturpedic tomorrow and find out. Now may I please sleep?"

"Sure. Guess who I ran into tonight?"

I realized there would be no peace until I guessed, and I began panicking. What if she rapped all night? If I don't get nine hours, I'm screwed. I hoped she'd go back to Canarsie soon. I already know how to give a blow job.

"Who?"

"India, I think there's an owl in heah."

"No, it was me. Who did you run into today?"

"Tony Messina."

"My ex? Oh god! Who was he with? How did he look? I

miss him so much! He was the love of my life!"

"Bullshit. You said you were bored with him and dug on his friend Chico."

"I was, and I did, but I realize now that Tony was the best thing that ever happened to me. I was a fool to let him go. I should've balled him. He claimed to have an eight inch cock."

Laura sat up. "What a bullshitter. His dick is maybe five inches, tops."

"*YOU FUCKED MY FAVORITE BOYFRIEND IN THE WHOLE WORLD?? HOW COULD YOU???*"

"India, it's not like it was last week. It was August. I didn't even know you then."

"*AUGUST? I WAS GOING WITH HIM IN AUGUST!! YOU FUCKED MY BOYFRIEND WHILE I WAS GOING WITH HIM??*"

"Well, *you* weren't fucking him! He told me he had DSB after makin' out withcu, and had to jerk off in the bathroom."

"You mean that's what he was doing in there? I thought he had digestive issues."

"Oh, he was backed up alright, just not the way you think. Anyways, he looks great. He has a new chick called Rainbow, and said to say hi. He remembas when you guys watched the last episode of The Fugitive. Says he doesn't remomba the ending cause he was outta the room at the time."

"Yes, and now we both know why. Jeez, can't guys control their urges? Couldn't he have waited a few minutes to beat off?"

"I'm not sure, Ind. I think if you let blue balls go, the stuff backs up and paralyzes your dick. At least, that's what Tony said. By the way, that singer from Blood, Sweat and Tears seemed interested in me tonight."

"Which one?"

"Don't get your knickas in a knot. It's not the one you like. Let's go to sleep. Tomorrow I'll teach you—ya know."

"That's okay, Laura, I already know how. Tell me one thing. How were you planning on teaching me the fine art of fellatio? You don't have a dick."

"I use a cuke. They feel so realistic, all bumpy and stuff."

"Yuck. Remind me never to eat one of your salads."

Jeez, Arn, sorry you're not here so I can practice on you. I

9/12/68

Dear Arn,

I'm happy to announce that Laura has moved back with her boyfriend. It was cool having someone to sleep with, but I'm tired of ironing hair. I wish I had long wavy hair like she does. We're never happy, are we? Tomato, tomahto, and all that shit. Maybe I should call the whole thing off. My parents don't like me, my sisters think I'm from another, far less groovy planet, and I don't know what to do with myself. I've had my summer of sex, drugs and rock, and am immobilized by a sheer lack of direction. College seems sophomoric and I'm too young to get married. This leaves more sex, drugs and rock. Do people actually sit around trying to make these types of decisions? It all seems inherently meaningless. If these are my only choices, I'm fucked anyway. Wasn't I supposed to get parental guidance in this area? Perhaps I'll move to India with the Beatles. I adore the food, I have the name, and some inner peace would be swell. Maybe if I knew what it was, I'd go after it. Is it what I feel on mesc? Is it forgetting reality, or dealing with it? What *is* reality anyway? Is it taking mesc, or being happy *not* taking mesc? Fuck it. I'm dropping acid and going to Nowhere. By the way, last week I had an abortion. Never believe a guy who claims sperm fall asleep when it's hot outside. They're lying through their testes. Miss you. I

OH DADS,
POOR DADS

10/11/68

Dear Arnie,
Just received your postcard from Madison. Wish I could've joined you at U of W, but right now I prefer tripping my brains out and hanging with lowlifes. We all have our priorities.

You'll never believe what happened! I found out last Sabbath that I'm Jewish! Oy gevalt! Mom came into the kitchen while I was eating lox, and dropped the J Bomb.

"Kiddo, we need to talk."

"What about, Mater?"

"Swallow. I have something big to tell you, and you might choke."

I sighed. "Okay, what is it?"

"Harry's not your father."

"Ma, quit kidding around."

"I'm serious. Harry is not your real father."

I was glad I'd stopped eating.

"That's impossible! Though come to think of it, last summer Aunt Pat hinted that Dad wasn't my father, but since she'd had four Manhattans, I figured she was going for the attention."

"That bitch! I wanted to be the one to tell you! I've never trusted women with large families. They inhale too much cleanser."

"Jesus, Ma, what difference does it make who told me? I still can't believe Steve Golden is my father."

"Hey, how do you know his name? Oh, I get it. Pat really spilled her guts, didn't she? Just because all her kids have the same father (although I have my doubts about the youngest. He looks like her plumber...")

"No one told me. I just knew."

"You knew? There are two billion men on the planet who could have fathered you, and you picked Steve's name out of a hat?"

"Two billion? Boy, you've certainly been busy."

"India, don't be crass. You know what I mean."

"All I know," I seethed, " is that Steve's name must have been floating just below the surface, like the elusive butterfly of parental fuck-ups. Is that what all those hours with Mazur were about? Were you trying to jog my memory?"

"No, that was because you walked in on Harry masturbating. But we did find out that you have sexual problems, so it wasn't a total loss."

"What???? I'll have you know I'm quite well adjusted sexually. Mazur is just jealous because I rejected him!"

"India, I'm shocked. I thought you were a virgin."

"A virgin? Mother, get real. This is 1968. There *are* no virgins. Really, someone needs to tell the Muslims. How come no one told me this news before, not counting Aunt Pat? Like when I was five? Didn't I have a right to know?"

"India, use your indoor voice. The Levines are downstairs. Do you want them to think we have problems?"

"Ma, they've lived here four years. If they don't know by now that we have problems, they must be subletting. How could Steve give me up?" I wailed. "Didn't he love me?"

"Yes, but he had issues."

"Yeah, he probably couldn't stand being around you! That's probably why Daddy left, too!"

"Don't lash out. Your father left because he wanted lots of little Catholics running around the house, and I didn't want kids. Er, more kids. Steve left because he's Jewish and can't handle responsibility."

"Mother, that's racist! Of course Jews can handle responsibility. Look at all the deli owners. I'm Jewish. God, how ironic! All those years I lied and told the kids at school I was Jewish, and now I actually am!"

Mom made a beeline for the medicine chest.

"India, you're hysterical. I'm getting the Librium."

"Arnie's gonna piss his pants when he hears about this."

"Here, swallow."

Mom held out a french-manicured handful of blue pills.

"Are you homicidal? Even *I* don't take that many pills at once!"

"You're upset, dear. They'll relax you."

"Fuck you. I'm going to live with Harry. Shit, I forgot. He's not my father. I can't live under the same roof with him!"

"That's absurd. Harry adopted you."

"Fine, I'm going to Daddy's."

"Over my dead body! You're not moving in with that—that Catholic!"

I stood and walked to the front door.

"Ma, how come it's okay for you to have relationships with these guys, but when I want to, you tell me what failures they are?"

"India, don't be absurd."

"That does it! I'm leaving! If I can't live with Daddy I'll find someone else. I'll go to Wisconsin and live with Arnie. He's a Psych major. Maybe he can help with my newfound trust issues. And we're both Jewish! *Oh dreydl dreydl dreydl* —"

Arn, I know the mother has to be Jewish for it to count,

but this is better than nothing. Just think, all that time I claimed to be a Jew I was lying, and now it turns out I was telling the truth! At least, it's the truth *today*. Back *then* it was a lie. Or was it? I'm so confused. I can't wait to start feeling Jewish. I love my people, and guilt is definitely one of my character flaws. By the way, I think I died in the camps in a previous life, because I also answer to the name Golda. Love and l'chaim, I

11/1/68

Arn,

I finally met my real dad last Friday at the Oak Bar. I wore paisley, he wore a hair shirt. Actually, Steve is somewhat entertaining, and we look very much alike.

"Hi, you must be Steve. Can we eat now?"

"Sure. Would you like a drink?"

"I don't ingest organic poisons. Besides, I dropped acid earlier."

"Uh oh, I hope you didn't burn your hands."

"Huh?"

"So, what would you like?"

"Whitefish salad on rye. Why did you abandon me?"

"Wow, way to cut to the chase. The truth is, the Navy needed me back."

"Steve, fifty thousand men fought in Korea. Surely they could have done without you."

"You're right. I had to get away from your mother. She was too controlling."

"You can say that again! I knew she was the culprit! Let me get this straight. You risked your life fighting in the Pacific to get out from under Mom's thumb and rejoined the Navy, where they won't let you piss without permission?"

Steve nodded.

"At the time, it seemed the preferable alternative."

"No shit! So why are you here now?"

"I wanted to see how you turned out, and whom you most resemble—me or Pam."

Oy. After an hour of 'why did you leave me, didn't you love me?' crap, I'd had it with family bonding. I was high and wanted to be with friends.

"Are you happy, Steve? Have you seen what you came to see?"

"Yes, but it's still early. Let's go to the Village and cruise for chicks!"

"I don't really swing that way, but how's about I take you to my fave hangout, Nowhere? They have outasite burgers."

"India, we just ate! Though now that you mention it, I could go for a pizza."

"With mushrooms?"

"Of course, dear. What other kind is there?"

I was actually starting to like the guy.

"Hey, I don't suppose you'd like to call me Dad."

"No, but I'll go to temple with you some time."

"Actually, I'm a Catholic now."

"What??? I've only been a Jew for five minutes! I was just getting used to it!"

"Sorry, hon, but my folks converted when they came to the States. They're first cousins."

That certainly explained a few things. Not only am I a Jew sans portfolio, but inbred as well. As Steve and I left the Plaza, I was infused with a warm inner glow, as if something misplace had been located. Or maybe I was peaking. Whichever, I was feeling magnanimous.

"It's been groovy meeting you, Steve. I'm glad you're not an asshole like Mom said."

"Same here. Come on, let's go hang out with beatniks."

"Actually, we're called hippies now. But if you pay for the cab, I'll recite poetry."

"Cool."

"There was a young boy from Nantucket —"

And so, the elusive butterfly of parental fuck-ups is safely netted for the moment. Or is it paternal fuck-ups? Prenatal? Life is such an anagram sometimes. Actually, it's sort of nice having a spare dad with disposable income and a wellspring of guilt. Sometimes I wish I'd been born into another species, though. Humans torment their kids with their insidious neuroses. Animals eat their young and get it over with. I

1/1/69

Dear Arnie,

Happy New Year!!!! It's great that we're still young and foolish enough to believe we might actually find happiness this year.

Steve has been calling a lot. After fifteen years apart, he's decided he wants to be my daddy. Well, he's too late—I already have a daddy. But he's fun to hang with, and if I sublimate my anger, we have a pretty decent time together. On Christmas, I saw Steve and Mom together in the same room for the first time since I've had memories. I felt like I was tripping, but I wasn't. I don't do drugs on religious holidays. I have, however, tripped every second day for the past year. Acid is my life. It helps me plumb the depths of my soul so I can feel serene, like the Maharishi. Miss you. I

LYDIA PHONE CALL # 1 – 1968

"Hello?"

"Hi, Mrs. Sarkesian, it's India. Is Lydia home?"

"She no can come to phone. She helping me skin rabbit."

"Oh, yuck! I mean, oh shucks. Listen, could I speak with her for just a minute? It's really important."

"I no think so. You bad influence."

"Oh no, Mrs. S. Lydia's my friend and I love her!"

"You keep her out too late! She young girl. Her papa get mad and he hit her."

"I'm so sorry, but staying out until ten when you're eighteen is not considered unusual in this country."

"Well we not from this country. We from Armenia."

"Ya know, I'll bet even Armenia is loosening up these days. After all, it *is* the sixties. Please, let me talk to Lyd. I have this problem–"

"You are pregnant? Lydia can no help sluts."

"No, nothing like that, but thanks for the vote of confidence. I need her advice on—er—what to cook for this party I'm having."

"Hold on. Lydia, it's that slut India. Don't be long. Your rabbit is drying out."

"Ind, hi! How come you never call anymore? We used to

be best friends."

"I *do* call, but I can't get past the warden. Your mom just called me a bad influence. Jesus, if she only knew! Wasn't that killer hash we smoked on Easter?"

"Yeah, outasite. It's such fun getting—er—*trying out new foods.*"

"Your mom is listening, right?"

"You betcha. Sounds great. How's Olga?"

"She's hanging with lezzies now, so I'm keeping my distance. I hope sleeping with me so often didn't turn her into one. Speaking of sex, Jesus and I split and I'm depressed. Why are guys such shits and why do we keep wanting them?"

"I guess we're addicted, Ind. *Just a sec, Ma. So to make basterma, you take the veal and pound it really thin, then....*"

"Hey, who're you calling a bastard!?"

"India, basterma is an Armenian dish. If I were Indian I'd be telling you how to make raita. Personally, I'm glad I don't have a boyfriend. I'm having enough trouble dealing vicariously with yours. My advice: Don't get involved with any more PRs, anyone else named after the son of God, or anyone under thirty. They're too unstable. Or anyone over thirty either, for that matter. You can't trust them."

"Swell, so I can only get involved with non-Hispanics who are celebrating their thirtieth birthdays. Where do I meet this eclectic group?"

"I don't know. School reunions, maybe? Better yet, OD a few times. The ER docs are all around 30, and they're doctors, too!"

"Seriously Lyd, I need a boyfriend. Why don't you?"

"I prefer livestock."

"Livestock? You're skinning a rabbit as we speak."

"Look, I promise not to eat any real pets. Besides, pets don't turn on you like guys do."

"Are you kidding? Last week Patches gave me a nasty scratch when I tried feeding her Windowpane. I never want kids. I've raised myself and that's enough. God, I'm glad school is nearly over. Just three more arduous months. How about those SATs? Jesus, could they give them any earlier in the day? I was still tripping heavily during the Reading Comprehension part. It was like 'Micronesia is an island off the coast of...hey, who finger-painted all over my Blue book?' You can see why I didn't do well."

"Don't worry, you're not going to college anyways, right? I thought you were gonna be a model."

"I was, but I'm too short and my nose is too big and my hair is stringy and–"

"... *so then you add oregano to the sauce and let it simmer for an hour.* India, you're too self-critical. You have a high IQ, you're gorgeous and you're tall."

"Lyd, you're 4'11". There are midgets taller than you. I'm only 5'5". Cheryl Tiegs is 5'10"!"

"Okay, then go to college. Listen, I've got to run. I think Ma is getting suspicious at the length of this recipe."

"Okay, but Lyd? Would you call Tony Messina and tell him I miss him and would be happy to view his eight-inch schwanz now?"

"I thought you didn't love Tony anymore. Didn't you call him a slimy Guinea with his brain up his stu gatz?"

"I say that about all my exes. Only the ethnicity changes. Besides, I really love Tony. But if he turns you down—or is it me he'd be turning down?—could you call Chico? I had such a crush on him while I was seeing Tony. And then there's Azteca—"

"Azteca? Are you that desperate?"

"Yes, actually, I am. I need to be held. I need to be touched. I need someone to tell me they love me."

"I love you, Ind."

"Thanks, but it only counts when guys say it."

"True. Well, bye. If you can get some bread together, let's score some Acapulco next week. *And be sure to preheat your oven. You don't want your buns getting burned.*"

"I wish. Bye, Lyd."

WOODSTUCK

8/30/69

Dear Lyd,

Guess what??? I went to Woodstock and fucked Ben Morrisey! Despite being grounded by mom for smoking hash, I snuck out and had the best time!

Remember Laura, the chick who fellates cucumbers? We were on the Thruway, trying to hitch a ride. We'd been there an hour and had tried everything possible, including the old Claudette Colbert routine, which doesn't work too well wearing bells. Desperate, I opted for Plan B, as in Boobs.

"Hey Laura, take off your shirt."

"You're not turnin' lezzie are you, Ind?"

"Oh for chrissake, I'm not gay. It's just that you have great tits and we may get picked up if you flash them."

"I dunno. There's something immoralistic about strippin' to get a ride. What if they think we're hoors or somethin'? What if we get murdered by drug-crazed hippies?"

"Laura, we *are* drug-crazed hippies. We're immune."

"Oh yeah."

Lyd, Laura is from Canarsie, and I understand maybe every fifth word she says, but with a few charades, we manage.

"Besides", I rationalized, " it's earthy to strip. Do you

think anyone at Woodstock will be clothed?"

"Okay, okay. I think your fulla crap but I'll do it anyways. Anything to get outta this heat!"

Laura whipped off her shirt and I was duly impressed.
It seems someone else was too, because we soon heard the
screech of brakes.

"Far out, it's a fuckin' limo! My tits are lethal weapons,
Ind!"

As we approached the car, I noticed that Laura made no
attempt to cover herself.

"Hop in!" said the driver, ogling Laura's tits. "I assume
you birds are headed to Woodstock."

We climbed into the air-conditioned car and sighed
blissfully.

"Yes, we're headed to Yasgur's farm to hear Ben Morrisey,"
I said. "I am *so* into him!"

"Yeah, we've just gotta see Ben. I have all his rekids and
.....eeeeeeek! India, look, it's Ben! Ben Morrisey is in dis car!
I think I'm gonna puke!"

Laura's outburst fed my head inappropriately. I touched
my third eye to bliss out and turned around. Sure enough,
there was Ben.

"Oh my God, Ben! I can't believe it's you! My name is
India and this is Laura. You may need a translator. She's
from Canarsie."

Ben offered his hand. "Pleased ta meetcha. I'm Ben
Morrisey."

"No shit! I mean, we know who you are. We just can't
figure out why you picked us up."

Ben chuckled. " What can I say? I'm a sucker for a nice
set o' hooters. Meet Ian. He's my chauffeur."

"So Ben, I guess you know where we're headed, seeing
as you're playing there on Sunday."

Ben nodded. "Actually, I live in the area, so I won't be
goin' to the festival right away. But I'd be happy to drop you

off, seein' as I need to buy a few groceries in town."

Laura gasped. "You do your own shoppin'?"

"Sure, lass. Don't you?"

"Yeah, but we ain't famous."

Ben chuckled. "Hell, everyone's famous up here. When I shop at the Healthatorium I see the same folks you pay thirty bucks to see. The town of Woodstock is much hipper than the stupid festival. Hey, why don't you blow off the first two days and come to my place?"

Whoa! My idol of idols and all around basically groovy alcoholic Irish rock star was inviting us home with him for the weekend! Oh wow!!!

"Sure, Ben. There's no one at the stupid concert we wanted to see except you. We don't care about Cocker or Havens. They're flashes in the pan. It's *you* we love, Ben, only you!"

"I'm countin' on it, lassies," Ben crooned, leering at Laura's tits.

The following day, the four of us were in Ben's playroom, playing.

"Okay, lassies, time to switch."

"But Ben, I was having such a good time with you. Do we really have to switch with Laura and Ian?"

"India, you know the rules. It's time for a new rubber."

"Okay, but I swear, I'll never get the hang of bridge. Personally, I prefer chess."

Ben strummed his guitar idly. "Speaking of chess, I have a set made of dark chocolate. It really challenges yer will-power when you've got the munchies."

At the mention of food my ears pricked up. "When are we hitting the Healthatorium? I'm famished!"

Laura glanced up from Omar Sharif's bridge book, where she was busy looking up the definition of rubber.

"I don't wanna go out! There's food heah! Besides, you just wanna see famous people!"

"Don't you?"

"Nah, I'm too cool for dat. I ain't impressed by fame."

"Laura, you are so full of shit. Who are we playing bridge with, street people?"

"You mean Ben? I don't consida him famous no more."

Ben grimaced. "Thanks a lot, lassie."

"How can you not consider him famous? You've known the guy less than a day."

"Yeah, but we know each otha in the biblical sense so it seems longa."

I looked at Ben. "You're kidding! You guys are making it? When? How? Laura was in bed with me all night!"

Laura snickered. " Rememba when I said I had to pee? Well, I snuck into Ben's room for a quickie."

"Ben, I'm shocked! When I snuck in you said you were too tired!"

"What can I say, Ind? I'm a sucker for big hoots."

"That's great!" I huffed. "So I'm stuck with Ian the chauffeur. Uh, no offense Ian, but you're no Ben Morrisey."

Ian smirked. "Yeah, I can get it up."

Ben looked at Laura. "Lassie, are you tellin' tales outta school?"

"No way. Besides, you had a semi. If only you hadn't had that last shot of Jack I know you coulda done it good."

I raised my hand. " Excuse me, but I have a few questions: a) How does Ian know that Ben can't get it up? and b) How can you prefer Laura to me? My ego is killing me!"

"It's not that I prefer Laura, lassie, it's just that she got to me first. As fer yer other question, Ian likes to watch."

"Whatever. Let's drop acid and go shopping!"

"India, yer a lass after my own heart. Maybe later we can make up fer last night."

Lyd, the Woodstock Healthatorium was packed with celebs. Every group not performing was there. But why?

I wondered. It's a health food store. What was the big attraction?

"Holy shit, Ind, dis place is far out! I can't believe all the groups in heah! Too bad I ain't no groupie. With my tits I'd have a field day."

"You know, yesterday you didn't think much of your tits. I'm the one who told you they had value. Now suddenly Ben is into them and you think they're God's gift. And whaddya mean you're not a groupie? Who were you fucking last night, the postman?"

"Ok, so I'm internin'. Man, dis is too much! Maybe we're hallucinatin' the whole thing. I'm goin' ova and touchin' Hendrix to see if he's real."

"Are you nuts? You can't just walk over and touch a big star. You wanna spend the night tripping in the Woodstock County jail?"

"No, but I gotta touch him. I promise to keep my shirt on."

"Well okay, but as long as your doing it, can you see if those plaster casts of his dick are accurate?"

"You want me to touch his cock? I can't do that, Ind. They'd lock me up for sure!"

"Fine, then I will. And I'll do it in a way he'll never suspect what I'm up to."

Ben walked over. "Hi there, lassies. What are you gals up to? There's a gleam in yer eyes."

"Hey, Bennie. India's gonna go touch Jimi's —er—cast."

"You must be hallucinatin', lass. Jimi has no broken bones."

"Ayeeeeeeeeee!" Laura was a goner, having entered the twilight zone of acid giggles. I hoped I wouldn't get sucked in, but I felt the first twinges, and figured I'd better get the Hendrix thing taken care of posthaste. I found him next to the broccoli, which was just about at crotch-level.

"Excuse me, Mr Hendrix. Could I reach around you to get some broc...oh, I'm dreadfully sorry! Your pants are green and I'm tripping and—"

"No sweat, mama. Come over to my pad later for a stir-fry that'll change your life."

"Thanks, I'll get back to you."

I returned to Laura and Ben. "See? I told you I could do it! He thinks I mistook his cock for a stalk of broccoli. God, he's huge!"

"Ayeeeeeeeee!"

"Laura, cut it out! I can't stand when you laugh that way. I can't control myself and—ayeeeeee!"

Two down, none to go. Ben turned beet red and split, which was even more amusing than the broccoli thing, seeing as he spends half his time on stage slumped over his mic from too much Jack. Nevertheless, people were beginning to freak. After all, this *was* a health food store.

"C'mon Laura, we've...gotta...cool it! Hee hee."

" I can't...help it...Ind, Ive...got...to...pee..bad! Hee hee!"

"Oh no, hee hee, not in here!"

"Yeah, ova heah, quick! Hee hee."

Laura yanked me into a corner filled with bread and squatted.

"*ON THE BREAD*? Laura, you're peeing all over the pita! Oh god! Peeing on the pita...it's too much! Ayeeeee!"

"Ind, I'm so embarrassed. Ayeee! Let's get outta heah."

We egressed with celerity.

"Whew! Fresh air at last! Hey, we're in the back of the store. Look at that line! I wonder what they're waiting for."

"I dunno, Ind, but I'm startin' to freak."

"Christ, Laura, do you have to display every single side-effect of acid? You've already laughed so hard you became incontinent, which still reeks by the way. And now you're paranoid. Thank god there aren't any tall buildings around."

"Oh wow, everyone's gettin' shots. I hate needles, Ind. I gotta get outta heah!"

"Wait! You don't have to get a shot. Let's just find out what type of shots they are."

"Oh god, they're green! Are we on Mars?"

"Mars is red, stupid. God, they *are* green! Uh, excuse me Mr. Morrison, but what's in those shots everyone's getting?"

"Green magma. It really lights my fire."

"It does?"

"Sure. Where do you think I got the idea for the song?"

"What is it again? Green smegma?"

"Magma, but you're not as far off as you think. Wanna cut in line?"

"No thanks. I don't need any green stuff coursing through my veins. It might clash with the purple stuff that's already in there."

Laura grabbed my arm. "Ind, look, Ben's gettin' a shot! So this is why the place is so populah. I wonder what kind of drug is in dem shots."

"Well we're not sticking around to find out. Let's split before we get charged for twenty bags of piss-drenched pita."

"I'm wit you. Let's go back to Ben's and get totally fucked up."

"You mean we aren't already?"

"Yeah, but the acid's wearin' off and Ben's got some killer hash. Don't tell, but last night I got the munchies so bad I ate the black queen off the chessboard."

"Far out! I've always wanted to eat a king."

Saturday I awoke to the sound of male shrieks, which isn't pretty. I thought there was a peacock getting laid next to my head, but it turned out to be Ben.

"Ohmygod! Ohmygod!"

"Ben, Ben, what is it? What is it?"

"I'm late, I'm late!"

"For a very important date?"

"Yes, lassie. We overslept!"

"That's okay. I feel really well rested. Those secanols

were far out. Look on the bright side. It's Saturday. We have a whole day left to spend together."

"Nae we don't, because its fuckin' Sunday! Shite! I was due onstage an hour ago. I'm ruined!"

"Jeez, those downers were better than I thought. Ben, you have the best drugs."

Ben tugged on my arm. " Get Laura. We have to get over to Yasgur's right now!"

"Don't panic, hon. Rock stars are known for being temperamental. Laura, get your tits out here. We're going to Woodstock!"

"*I'll be right there, Ind. I have to get this green stuff outta my hair.*"

"What green stuff? Oh Ben, you didn't! And in her hair?"

"Aye, it's the shot. That's why we get them, so we can come in colors. Where do ya think Mick got the idea?"

"Yuck. Green was my favorite color 'til now."

"Never mind. Let's split."

And so we finally got to Woodstock—or what was left of it. Ben surveyed the detritus with tears in his eyes.

"Oh, India."

"Jesus Ben, all that's left is mud, trash and that couple fucking in the first aid tent."

Laura chimed in. "Hey, should I take my top off again? Maybe it'd bring people back."

"Laura, get a grip. Your tits are nice, but they're not *that* nice. On the other hand, they might make Ben feel better. Ben, crawl out of the mud and get over here. Laura has a surprise for you."

We didn't see any performances, but we're great friends with Ben now, and we discovered the secret of the Healthatorium, as gross as that is. All in all, not a bad weekend. Next weekend I'm going to Jimi's for a stir-fry. Broccoli's always been my fave veggie, even if it *is* green. I

9/3/69

Dear Lyd,

The summer of love is over, and I assume the winter of my discontent is on the horizon. I have no boyfriend, no career and no goals, except to score acid. The problem is, when I drop acid, all I think about is having no boyfriend, no job and no goals, except scoring more acid. Oh, what the fuck. Peace be with you, and mazeltov for getting a job with the phone company. At least one of us is on the way up. I

NOWHERE

7/24/70

Dear Lyd,

Why must you go to Armenia every summer? You're missing all the fun, and I'm afraid the nuns are brainwashing you. Don't listen to them. Sex is the best. I'd be happy to send you a vibrator to counteract any evil programming—batteries sold separately.

I've done nothing but trip and fuck this whole summer. Read and weep.

On July 21st, three men landed on the moon and I went into orbit. I'd just gotten to Nowhere, my fave Village club, when I felt the acid kick in. Lots of rockers hang at Nowhere, which is why I do. Most of the waitresses are groupies. Kaylie has made it with every member of Blood, Sweat & Tears, and Tina did three Stones at once. I've thought about becoming a groupie, but I'm not ambitious enough. Besides, rockers are boring. All they do is flick their hair and admire themselves. I'd like to fuck someone famous, but power is the ultimate aphrodisiac and all the cute Kennedys are dead, so fuck it.

My buddy Pete smiled as I squeezed into the booth beside him, his gleaming teeth and black skin evoking Al Jolson. I was about to break into a chorus of 'Mammy' when my friend Sue walked over. I freaked.

"Pete, help! Sue's been shot! She has blood all over her!"

"India, relax. She spilled her burgundy, that's all."

As Sue flung her ass-length hair to the side and sat down, I flirted briefly with the idea of a becoming a lez, but after visualizing the grotesqueries involved in eating Sue out, I decided against it.

"Sue, it's so groovy seeing you! How's Bay Shore? Wow, I love your skirt! What color do they call that?"

"White."

"Ah, but white is the presence of all color. Or is that black? Ooooh, you're undulating."

Sue grinned. "Got anymore, Ind?"

I removed a small sheet from my pocket. Sue downed it with the dregs of her wine and glanced at her skirt, hoping to see what I was seeing. She wouldn't have long to wait.

A short while later I felt myself growing muddy, as if my memory banks had been switched off. This had never happened before and I was concerned. What if I lost my memory forever? Was this a side effect of acid? Shit, I couldn't even remember *that*! I decided to run a test, and tried to concentrate on what Pete was saying.

"Pete, what did you just say?"

"Can't you hear me, Ind?"

"The music is awfully loud. So what did you just say?"

"When?"

I began to panic. "Just now! What was your last sentence?"

"I was talking about the Beatles' concert at Shea where I balled three chicks at once. Two were black and one was white so they called themselves the Oreos and..."

"Thanks, that's all I wanted to know."

Whew, that's right, he was telling that stupid Oreos story and—

"Uh Pete, sorry to interrupt again, but what did I just say?"

"When?"

"Just now, when you told about the Oreos?"

"You said that's all you wanted to know. India, what's up?"

"Oh, nothing. I'm just having a little trouble retaining dialogue."

"You're joking!" Sue giggled. "You can't remember what you just said? Far out! Ooohh, something's tickling me inside. I had chicken for dinner. Maybe they left some feathers on it! Ayeeeeeee!!!!!"

It was obvious that Sue had gotten off. But I'd dropped and hour earlier than she had. This meant we were at different stages of our trips. Could we still communicate? Did it matter?

"Sue, how's Mike? You two still an item?"

"Huh? Oh yeah, we're still getting it on, but his slut girlfriend Luz is suspicious and we had to cool it for a while. Anyways, I'm going after one of the Dead. Ever heard of Jerry Garcia?"

"Yeah, he's ugly."

"Well, it's not him. Hahahahaha."

Sue was overcome. But why was she laughing? Has she said something funny? Had I lost my sense of humor along with my memory? I figured I'd better laugh, just in case.

"Heh, heh, that's funny Sue. Tell me another one. Heh heh."

"Fuck you. You're faking. Those aren't acid giggles."

"Well, what you said wasn't funny."

"What did I just say, smartass?"

"I CAN'T REMEMBER!!!!!"

Pete stuck his face between us. "Use your inside voices, kiddies. Remember where you are."

The trouble was, I *didn't* remember, so I toyed with various possibilities. Was I home? No, this wasn't my room. Was I at work? No, because a) I wouldn't be stoned at work and b) I didn't have a job. At least I didn't remember having one.

What did I *do*, anyway? Then I saw Pete and Sue and knew I must be at Nowhere. What a relief!

Sue began moving her index finger up and down, pointing to a spot in the air. I looked and saw nothing, but it was what *Sue* was seeing that mattered.

"Sue, are you hallucinating?"

"Nah, I'm flicking letters off the tips of my finger."

"Hey, that's *my* hallucination. You stole it!"

"Tough shit. It's mine now. It's so weird, seeing the little letters drop off. I can summon any letter and it will drop right off my fingertip."

"Yeah, I know. Let me try. Hey, it still works! Let's both do it!"

And there we sat, fingers bobbing to some invisible rhythm, while I tried tuning back into the conversation.

"Pete, what did you just say?"

"I was telling Joe that I really like the new Traffic album. Winwood is far out."

"Yeah, I dig him, too. He's so cute! I wish he'd walk in here right now so I could take him to my place."

"Yeah, wouldn't that be a gas?"

"Wouldn't what be a gas?"

"What you just said."

"What did I just say?"

"That you wish Winwood would come to Nowhere."

"Oh, yeah."

"You know who I'd like to ball? Linda Ronstadt. I love some meat on a woman. She was in here the other night but I lost my nerve. Oh well, she probably doesn't dig black dudes anyway."

"Who doesn't dig black dudes?"

"Linda Ronstadt."

"What about her?"

"I said I'd like to fuck her."

I grinned wickedly. "I know someone who fucked her."

"Really? Details!"

"What details? Pete, did I just say something?"

"Jesus India, why do you drop that stuff if you can't remember anything?"

"What stuff?"

"Acid. Oh, never mind. Go back to twiddling your fingers."

I did, but I was worried now. I couldn't retain a thought for more than five seconds. What if I never remembered anything ever again? What if I'd totally fucked up my memory? I began hyperventilating and looked at Sue.

"Sue, how's your memory?"

"Huh? Who are you?"

Oh God. I turned to Pete.

"Pete, listen hon. I'm having an teeny problem here. I can't remember anything and I really need your help. Tell me if you think I retain more in a few minutes than I do now. That way I'll know I'm coming out of it. Hey Pete, listen hon. I'm having an teeny problem here and I really need your help. Tell me if..."

"India, you're repeating yourself. "

"I am? I am?"

"Yes, yes. You just asked me twice to help you."

"Help me what?"

Pete put his arm around me protectively.

"Don't worry kiddo, I'll help you."

Just then I spied a really hot guy walking towards us. He looked familiar but I couldn't place him.

"Hey Pete, who's the hunk? I'd love to fuck his brains out."

"You already have. That's your boyfriend, Dan."

"I knew he looked familiar! Danny, baby, let's make like atoms and split. Let's get into the back seat of your 'Vette."

"My 'Vette doesn't have a back seat. Besides, I have to get back to work."

"But you just got here!"

"Whaddya mean? I've been here for three hours."

"Three hours???!!!"

"Yes, and you've been asking what everyone said the whole time. See you later, babe."

I glanced anxiously at Sue, wondering if time had passed her unnoticed as well.

"Hey, Sue, what time is it anyways?"

"It's time for time."

"No, really, what fucking time is it?"

"Around two, I guess."

"Is your memory fucked up?"

"Nope, I remember every moment. Who did you say you were again?"

Oy. "Hey, Sue, you hungry?"

"Hunger is an evil emotion. It leads to carnivorous behavior and disgusting waste products."

" Sue, hunger isn't an emotion, it's a biological need. How about a nice slice of mushroom pizza?"

"OK, but I'm buying. My way of paying you back for the killer acid."

"Groovy. Hey Sue, you hungry?"

As we left Nowhere to go somewhere, I realized what's truly important in life, Lyd—good friends and mediocre pizza. Love, I

8/1/70

Dear Arn,

I've *got* to stop doing acid. I don't mind not being able to think if that's what I've set out to do, but if I'm incapable of thinking about whether I'm incapable of thinking, that's unthinkable. I hope I've made myself clear. Shalom. I

THE PLATINUM FACTORY

10/3/70

Dear Lyd,

After much brownnosing, I've landed a job at the Platinum Factory, doing set-up. I'm also dating a married man. (Don't scold). Irv is an engineer and is teaching me to mix. I'm dyslexic, but I'm faking it because I love Irv, even though he's old. Twenty-eight is nearly thirty! Irv has promised to leave his wife when I turn twenty-one. She's preggers with their second kid, but I can wait.

Earlier today I was setting mikes for a Latin session that Irv was mixing, and was in the same room as Jack Brazil, the Conga King. Cubans really know how to party, Lyd. I can see why Lucy was so into Ricky. Anyway, I took a hit of grass when the bong came around, and was instantly fucked. I couldn't concentrate, and knew I could no longer work. Afraid of pissing Irv off, I took a swig of Bacardi and immediately went into esophageal spasm, whereupon the Conga King flew to my side and pounded me on the back.

"Now jew weel fill better. Jew dunt drink mucho, jes?"

"Jes", I croaked. God, how humiliating! Jack Brazil was finally touching me and I was choking! Not that I *wanted* him to touch me. I'm totally in love with Irv. After I got my wind back, I weaved over to the old man.

"Hey Irv, I..."

"Hold on a sec, India. I'm on the phone. Yes, Eileen, me too. Okay, how about seven at L'Hermitage? Yes, I'll bring some, don't worry. I know you like protection. See you later. Bye."

"Hey, who's Eileen? Bring some what?"

"Er, that was the new receptionist. I said I'd meet her for a drink and fill her in on our employees. She suggested I bring a couple of, er, messages, so she can see how I like them written."

"Oh, okay. Listen baby, I'm fucked up from the weed. Can you find someone to cover me?"

"Okay, but don't make this a habit. You wanna get your skinny ass fired?"

"Oh Irv, I know you'd never let that happen. We're getting married, remember? Then we can be together 24/7!"

"Peachy."

Riiiinnnnnnggggg!

"Irv speaking. Oh, hi Sharon. Yeah, I'm a little busy at the mo. Dinner? Sure! I should get out of here by 8:30. Can you save your appetite? Oooooh, me too. See you later, sugar."

My face fell. "Hey, I thought *we* were having dinner!"

Irv shook his head. "Sorry, that was the new bookkeeper. I told her I'd take her out and explain the way we, er, bill clients. Okay, Jack, let's take it from the top."

Riiinnnggg!

"Hold on, guys. I've got to take this. Hi honey, how's it going? Contractions? But you're not due for a month! It's probably Braxton Hicks—uh, yeah, I'll be home, but I'm running late. I know, I wanted to be there, too. Can't you call your mother? Well, how about 911? Okay, try not to push and I'll be home around midnight. I love you, babe."

I hung on every word, Lyd. Jeannie was about to have

the kid, and he'd finally be able to leave her.

One toke over the line, I wandered across the all to Studio B to see my favorite leprachaun, Ben Morrisey. Ben's recording a new album, but it's over budget cuz he isn't sober all that often. He's really cute, though, and if it weren't for Irv... Oh well, been there, done him.

Ben lifted his head off the audio console.

"India, my pet, it's great seein' ya again! Is that yer twin sister?"

"No, there's no one here but me. And how are *you* today?" I asked, already knowing the answer.

"Oh, ya know me, lass. I'm always cheery. Do you like my new single? It's about dyin' and comin' back as a pet."

"It's lovely. It has a good beat and it's easy to dance to. I give it a 95."

Ben stood and pressed against me. "Girl, I love that mini yer wearin'. Wanna come into the loo for a sec?"

I figured Ben needed help with his aim. "Okay, but hurry. Irv is waiting."

"That's okay, lass. I still get off quick these days."

I pulled away as if slapped. "Hey, what am I supposed to do in there?"

"Suck me off, of course. It's not really sex, after all. Everyone wants to. You should feel honored."

I did, to a point.

"Sorry, I'm not a groupie. I know we fucked at Woodstock, but I can't stand blowing guys. It's messy and I hate the smell."

"Ya wear such short skirts, I figure you were askin' for it", Ben whined.

"Nope, I'm simply making a fashion statement. As for last summer, I was a kid. I'm dating a married man now, which ages a person. Now get back to work!"

Ben walked away, dick rebuffed, crooning something about how pets may have been our spouses in a former life.

Then he dropped like a stone.

"Hey, Ben, you okay man?"

Ben had passed out once again. Sighing, I returned to Studio A, fuming over the fact that my evening was fucked socially, and wondering if Irv should take a job with shorter hours. Jack's face lit up when he saw me. "India, jou're yus in time! We're wrapping!!"

It was Friday night and was lonely in advance. I figured I'd head over to Nowhere and drop some acid, wondering briefly if I should have sucked Ben off. It would have made a great story for the grandkids.

Just then, Irv rushed in. "It's a girl! I have a daughter!"

"Wow, that's groovy, hon. So I guess you won't be working late with those women tonight after all."

"Why not? Jeannie's in the hospital and there's nothing I can do."

"That's not the point. Don't you want to see your kid?"

Irv shrugged. "I'll be living with her for the next eighteen years. What difference does one day make?"

I freaked. "Whaddaya mean, eighteen years? I though you were asking for a divorce after the baby came."

"Oh, right, what was I thinking? See ya, babe. I've got work to do."

And so, the waiting game begins. I hope Irv leaves Jeannie soon, cuz I'm not getting any younger. Guess I'll find something to eat. *Or* someone.

Love, me

PS

An hour after I wrote the above, I dined with the Conga King, and who should we run into but Irv and the bookkeeper, necking in the rear booth. Needless to say, Irv and I are no more. He was a slimy Sephardic Jew with his head up his stugatz, anyway. At least I have my Lydia. Please move back to NY. I'm lonely and I have things to show you, like my new black vibrator. I'd give up men altogether, but vibrators can't move furniture. Love, Ind

1/22/71

Dear Arn,

How could I have dated a married guy? They never leave their wives, and after they've dated you, you become their surrogate wife and they commit adultery once removed on *you*. Now I have trust issues (again), and will never believe another word out of a guy's mouth. (Except for yours, of course.) I hear Irv is dating someone new, also named Jeannie. How convenient. If he calls out the wrong name while he's coming, it's still the right name. I think I need more therapy, Arn. I'd become a Buddhist, but I'm not into self-immolation. Perhaps I should start dropping acid again, but it's so 60's. I mean, how many talking water beds must one encounter before the thrill is gone? Don't get me wrong. I know that what I've seen while tripping is real. It's just that I've seen enough. My hallucinations have become predictable. I was actually starting to have boring trips. Is that an oxymoron? Am I? (A moron, that is.) I think that when you're no longer interested—or interesting—on acid, being straight is gonna be either ten times better or ten times worse.

I miss Irv. I miss Jimi and Janis. I miss you! I'm nearly twenty-one? When do the good times start? Have they started for you? The bitch of it is, in twenty years I'll look back and remember *these* as the good times. How fucked is that? Peace, India

NEWSCREAM

3/4/71

Dear Arnie,

In an effort to aid my ongoing search for enlightenment, I attended my first Primal Therapy session today a) because Danny's new girlfriend is in the group and I wanted to check out the competition and b) because I read Janov's book and felt I was ready to re-experience the trauma of the birthing process. Now I'm thinking my mom's dark tunnel may have been an easier commute.

As I entered the Newscream Center, a hot chick walked over.

"Hi, I'm Jeannie and I love you."

So this was Danny's new old lady. Wow. Tall, nice tits, your basic nightmare. But she was so old—at least thirty. I can't believe people still do it when they're over thirty. Aren't chicks all dried up by then? Hey, maybe it was some old fart that invented KY. Either that, or a horny Kentuckian.

"Hi, I'm India. How's it hanging?"

"Hi, India. In this group we always tell the other people we love them."

"But I don't love you. I don't even know you."

"I knooooowwwww. It's just something we say. I don't love you, either. I mean, Jeez, you're Irv's ex. Now hug me!"

"Wait a sec. You sound pissed. If you love Irv, you should

be happy we broke up. I don't feel like hugging anyone who emits negative vibrations."

"Of course I'm emitting negative vibrations. That's why I'm here. Irv said he'd give me a baby, but it's been a year and the clock is ticking. I want a baby now! You see that guy over there?" Jeannie pointed to a balding man. "I'm planning on having his kid. He doesn't know it yet but I'm seducing him this weekend."

So much for any juicy Irv gossip. Jeannie had obviously moved on. At ten we all filed into a small, soundproof room. Several chairs formed a circle surrounding a large, over-stuffed recliner, filled by a large, over-stuffed broad around forty. She looked lovingly into each face, but when she got to mine I knew she was faking it.

"Hi, I'm Sandra and I love you."

"And we love *you*, Sandra!" replied the group, causing me to flash back to a movie on the Hitler Youth I'd recently seen.

"Before we begin, let's turn and hug the person to our left."

I was afraid to look. What if it was someone old and smelly? But no, it was only the unwitting father of Jeannie's future kid, and he wasn't bad, despite his bald pate. I hugged him back and thought hey, who says *she* has to get him?

"Hi, I'm Stephen and I love you." Yum, this was getting better and better.

"Hi, I'm India and (oh what the fuck) I love you, too."

While we were hugging, I was on the lookout for moaning or a semi from Stephen, but when we broke apart he was sobbing.

"Jesus, what's wrong?"

"Nothing" he snuffled. " It's just that you remind me of my little sis, the one I fucked before entering therapy."

I jerked away as if slapped. He's all yours, Jeannie, I thought. Still, it would've been a nice compliment if the perv had gotten a boner during our embrace.

"Okay, group, hug time is over. Who would like to have the first Primal?"

A short man, whose burnt orange bells clashed nastily with a red and pink striped shirt, raised a pudgy arm.

"Yes, Stuie, what's motivating you to scream today?"

"Well Sandra, last weekend I took this new girl Carol I'm dating to see Elton John. I paid for the tickets, I paid for dinner, and I even sprang for some 'ludes so the sex would be more intense, and she wouldn't fuck me!" Sandra glanced menacingly at Stuie. "Uh, sorry. I love you, Sandra."

Tears were streaming down Stuie's puffy cheeks. "Anyways, when I asked her why she wouldn't, she said she's from Staten Island and the girls there are saving themselves for marriage, just like in third world countries. I felt so unattractive."

"It must have been very painful for you, Stuie, being rejected by some chick who claims she's a virgin, even though she's probably fucked the entire football team at Bishop Laughlin."

"Well yes, it was Sandra. I'm hurt! I'm angry! I'm—eeeeeeekkkkk!"

One down, nine to go.

"Good boy. Let it all out! Regress to the day you were born! Feel the pain of the birth canal!"

"Eeeeeeekkkkkk!"

"That's great. Now group, does anyone have anything constructive to say to Stuie when he finishes screaming?"

A middle-aged woman raised her hand.

"Yes, Agnes?"

"Sandra, I'm feeling angry at Stuie! Who does he think he is? When I was a girl we were respected for saving ourselves for our husbands. We were proud to be virgins, though between you and me, I wish I could've slept around a bit before I married George. His penis is so small. I know I have no real basis for comparison, but his fingers are larger. I've never enjoyed myself sexually and—eeeeekkkkkkk!"

Stuie quit screaming and gave Agnes the hairy eyeball.

"Hey, Agnes is interrupting my Primal! That's not cool."

"Now Stuie, you know we don't stop up our feelings in here. That's why we don't eat or smoke during our sessions. Please feel free to continue screaming."

"Aw, never mind. I only regressed as far as high school, anyways. But I still feel gypped. I'm angry at you, Agnes!"

"Eat me, Stuie. Eeeeeekkkkk!"

As I listened to all this shrieking, I wondered what would happen if a gang of thugs broke in and cut off our extremities, one by one. I mean, we were already screaming. Who'd notice?

"Okay, does anyone have any business they'd like to discuss?"

This was my big chance, Arn. I was paying twenty-five bucks and was determined to get my money's worth.

"Actually Sandra, you don't know me but I've got a problem I need to discuss."

"Yes, China, go ahead."

"It's India and I love you. My problem is my mom. See, she was never around when I was a kid and she didn't care about me. She sent me away a lot, and each time I came home she'd send me someplace else. Plus, I have two fathers, neither of whom I feel close to, and my self-esteem is in the gutter..."

"Oh no, not another 'poor me, my mommy never loved me' Primal! I'm so tired of people complaining about their parents, I could scream."

I turned to see who had the audacity to interrupt my first group share, and came face to face with Jeannie, who continued her diatribe on wimps.

"Why, my mother left when I was six months old, and I was raised by my granny who beat me twice a day—once

before taking her hormones, and once after. My uncles began showing me their things when I was ten, and when I
got my period they started humping me. Then when I was
eighteen my mom decided she wanted me and I went back
to her. You know why? Because I loved her and she did the
best she could, even if she fucked up my whole entire life.
Plus, she had no dick, which was a definite plus."

"Jeannie, I though we were friends! How can you attack
me like this?"

"Why should we be friends? Because we fucked the
same guy? By the way, Irv was married when you dated
him. Betcha didn't know that! While you were together, he
was fucking three other chicks, and I was one of them!"

"Pardon me, Jeannie", Stuie chimed in, "but it sounds like
you're angry at India when you should be angry with Irv."

"Shut up, you moron! You don't know what you're talking
about. You don't even know how to dress. Irv loves me! He
may fuck other women but that's only because I'm away on
business."

"Listen Jeannie", I said. "I'm no longer into Irv. I wish
you guys the best. However, I would like to finish what I
was saying about my moth..."

"I'm so angry at you, India. First you bring up your
stupid mother, and now you're forcing me to relive Irv's
infidelities. I can't believe you'd be so cruel, so insensitive,
so—eeeeeekkkkkk!"

Jesus, I thought. How come everyone is having a Primal
except me? I decided to be assertive.

"Would everyone please shut the fuck up? I was in the
middle of a share. As I was saying, my mother didn't give
two shits about me and..."

Sandra began pounding the arms of her recliner. "I'm angry at you, mommy! Bad mommy! I hate you, you lying sack
of shit! Eeeeekkkkk!"

The room started to sound like a kennel on July 4th. Still,

I knew I had to express my contempt for the caterwauling assholes horning in on my share.

"Sandra, I mean no disrespect, but there's something weird going on here. Each of us paid twenty-five bucks to scream our lungs out so you can guide us through the choppy straits of clinical depression onto an island blossoming with mental rose gardens. Instead, you have a Primal on our time, while we watch with empty pockets. This doesn't seem fair."

"We all love Sandra", said Jeannie, cradling Sandra. "We don't care if she has *ten* Primals a day!"

Stephen sidled over to Sandra and hugged her tightly. "Yeah! Before my Primals I was an animal. Sandra taught me to love everyone, not just nubile six-year olds..."

"Stephen, snap out of it! Remember what we discussed."

Stephen wiped spittle from his lips.

A large, black woman, heretofore silent, began sobbing loudly. Sandra quit ululating and looked at her.

"Yes Rose, what would you like to emote today?"

"Oh God, I'm having the worst pains! I'm so nervous about my son Jamal's wedding to that honky, tattooed bitch he met at the parole office. She ain't nothin' but trouble. Oooh, my gut..."

"Okay Rose, you know how get those feelings out." Sandra grabbed the trash pail. "That's right, bring those wicked feelings right out of your gullet!"

I was halfway down the hall when I heard the first retch. Arn, I can take yelling, screaming, even ululating, but I'm not paying to watch someone puke.

As I boarded the 104 bus, I realized that despite my failure to communicate effectively today, I'd actually learned something from the Primal Therapy experience: a) I learned that it's stupid and I hate it b) Lennon must really have been fucked up to benefit from that shit c) Jeannie can have Irv, and d) Sandra's too busy having Primals to be an effective leader, although I think Stuie has potential. As for moi, I think I'll return to more conservative forms of psychothera- py. Maybe you and I can get married. Just think, a husband and shrink rolled into one. I'm feeling happier already! I feel like— eeeeeekkkkk! I

RADIO DAZE

6/15/72

Dear Lydia,

Today was my first day mixing at WBCA Radio, and I've already pissed off Uncle Mikey, the biggest DJ on the planet. I simply expressed a preference for the WMCA Good Guys, and all hell broke loose.

"Whadaya mean you like Gary Stevens better than me? I'm much more famous than him! Open my mike!"

Being that it was my first day, I had only a vague idea of what I was doing. Panicked, I pressed every button on the audio console, hoping to hit the right one. Eventually I did.

"Hey there, nieces and nephews, its 6:22 on a wonderfunderful Monday, and that was Gilbert O'Sullivan crooning his latest. Welcome to the Groovatorium, where I'm taking requests on the Groovaphone. If you're the 99th caller from Bay Shore, I'll play your fave vibration in the nation. Okay, start callin'!"

Mikey began gesturing at his throat. Was he choking on his own vapid verbiage, I wondered? Oh goody! But I didn't hear any gagging. In fact, I didn't hear anything, and I had the feeling it was my fault. I shrugged helplessly.

"Cut the mic you little cun—excuse me, folks. We have a new employee who doesn't know her ass from her elbow. India dear, please turn my mic off."

I flipped a switch.

"Thanks, you fucking bitch. First you insult me by throwing the Good Guys in my face, and then you embarrass me by deliberately leaving my mic open! You're not long for this place, mark my words!"

"Uh, Uncle Mikey? I think you're mic's still hot. Can you show me how to kill it?"

"It's that switch over there, dear. The one that says Mikey's Mic on it."

I flipped a switch.

"Sorry Mikey, I'm new here and—"

"It's *Uncle* Mikey! I'm ruined! I said 'fuck' on the air! I'll get you for this!"

"But Uncle Mikey, I didn't know what you wanted."

"But I gestured!"

"You pointed at your throat. I thought you were choking!"

I flipped a switch and Mikey cocked his head.

"Jesus, there's dead air. Quick, play something!"

"I have a kazoo in my purse."

"No you imbecile, play a record!"

I flipped a switch.

"In a little while from now, if I'm not feeling any less sour..."

"Christ, we just played that song! We're only supposed to play it three times an hour, not four! This is all your fault, Pakistan."

"It's India."

"Never mind. Get out! And now Teddy Behr with the news."

"Thanks, Mikey. Our top story tonite is the second-rate break-in at the Watergate Hotel. It will probably amount to nothing, but we have a reporter on the way..."

Jesus, Lyd, what an asshole! How could Mikey humiliate me, live on the air? I hate radio. Maybe there's still time to become a gyno. I should've gone to Amsterdam with Laura to deal hash when I had the chance. I'm too responsible now, and two hundred a week is a lot of bread. I'll just have to stick it out. I hear the FM jocks are a lot hipper. Love, I I

8/23/72

Dear Lyd,
I met one of the FM jocks today—Bob Malloy. The voice is crushed velvet, the hair black silk, the eyes blue as opals, and he makes twice what I make! I think I'm gonna like radio after all. I

6/10/73

Dear Lyd,
   Bob and I have been married for six months. During that time I've been laid off, Bob was fired for smoking hash with Lennon on the air, and we've been living in Ypsilanti because Bob had a job lead here. Lyd, I've married an alcoholic. We dated for three months before our marriage. How could I have missed the signs? I mean, once in awhile Bob would drink a pint of Jack, and he did like having a bottle or two of wine with dinner. At times he even downed a six-pack before work because he claimed it made his voice smoother, but I never figured the guy for a drunk.
   Last week I put my foot down. Bobby needed a gig, so we got on the train and headed for Chi-town. After a few hours I started getting hungry. This is when I got the bad news—we didn't have a cent. Nevertheless, Bobby said he'd go to the bar car and find us something to eat. While he was gone I reran the shower scene from "Psycho" in my head, wondering how feasible it might be to reenact—with Bob as the stabee. I wondered if half a bottle of Valium would kill my appetite—or Bob. I wished fervently that I'd married Arnie instead, but with him entering grad school and my neurotic need to latch onto famous people to validate

myself, we never found the time. I cursed the day I'd met Bob, and vowed to stay away from good-looking drunks in the future.

"I'm back honey, and I brought you some chow."

"You've been gone for an hour and all you brought back were eight packets of ketchup!?"

"Yep. Eat hearty."

It was then that the smell hit me.

"Bob, where did you get the fucking beer???!!!"

"Sssh, there are Mormons across the aisle. I slipped the bartender the new Traffic album and he gave me a beer. What's the biggie?"

"Jeez, what do I have to do to get a sandwich? Blow the guy?"

"India, don't be crass."

"I'm always crass when I'm starving. It pisses me off to be hungry! Hey, how do you know the people across from us are Mormons?"

"Uh, they look Mormon, is all."

"Oh, just go away and leave me in peace, alright?"

It was dinnertime, and while the Mormons picnicked on fried chicken and potato salad, I wiped the drool from my mouth. If only I had a tiny piece of chicken, or a few Doritos to boost my sodium levels—

"Why are you crying, dear?"

It was the Mormon chick.

"Oh, it's nothing. I didn't get much sleep last night because our mansion was robbed and the greyhounds escaped and—and I'm so frightfully hungry."

"Here, grab a breast."

"I'm not *that* hungry..."

"Of chicken, dear. I fried it myself. And please, call me Ella."

"Thanks, Ella. I believe I will have some. You're very generous and have lovely children."

"Get real. My kids are pains in the ass and ugly as sin.

Just because we're Mormons doesn't mean we're perfect. Why, I was in the bar before, and this tall, good-looking young man told me I was beautiful, so we went to the restroom and I gave myself to him. Afterwards I bought him a beer."

Lyd, it seems my asshole husband was prostituting himself for free drinks. I was stunned, and vowed to file for divorce the minute we hit Chicago, which I did. Alone again, naturally. I

4/4/74

Dear Arnie:

Well, my first marriage is over. Now that I have one under my belt I can relax. Next time, I want someone more mature—someone like you. By the way, Lydia is now dating Bob. She dates all my castoffs. Maybe it's like dating me once removed. Love you madly. I

THEY GET LETTERS

10/11/74

Dear Arnie,

Thanks for the birthday card. I was surprised to learn you're studying at the Sorbonne. I guess that lets out dinner at Hunan Palace this Friday. By the way, congrats on your recent marriage. I wish you both the best. Marriage sucks, Arn, so don't get complacent.

How are your parents? I've always loved them, even though they hated me because I'm a shiksa. Now that I'm half Jewish, perhaps they will rethink things.

I've been trying lots of new therapies lately. I've done Freudian, Primal, Reichian, Orson Bean's orgone stuff (that's where you go into a box and gag yourself), and biofeedback. Nothing is helping. Plus, I have all these extra parents. My adoptive dad Harry recently married a hand model (the lazy bitch—god forbid she should wash a dish), and my pop, Steve has moved in with my ex because he's always wanted a son. Does this make Bob my stepbrother? As for mom, she's living with the surgeon who lifted her jowls last year. I'm happy to say, he offers a 20% discount to family.

Please advise if you hear of a therapy that might work for me, as gagging has lost its allure. I miss you. Too bad you're married. Call soonest if this changes.

WENDY VEGA

We're destined.
    Love, I

11/7/74
Dear Olga,
    How great hearing from you! Congrats on your recent marriage. I'm sure you and Linda will be very happy. I admit I used to wonder about your sexuality. You groaned when you massaged me, and you never fucked guys. When you joined the Marines and got stationed in San Fran, I figured the worst. But hey, no problem. I'm open-minded, and your plan to be inseminated with sperm from MENSA sounds doable. But what if you guys split? Judges usually award custody to the mother, but you're *both* mothers (no offense). Maybe the judges out there are used to this situation. Let me know all outcomes.
    As for moi, I've been divorced for nearly a year. No serious crushes at the mo, but I'm always on the lookout. By the way, thanks for giving your maid of honor my number. I think I'll stick to guys for now, but if this changes I'll notify you soonest.
    After two years of unemployment, I've been rehired by WBCA. Uncle Mikey had a stroke, and since Bob is no longer there, nepotism isn't a problem. Alas, the format has changed, but I could probably use some religion at this point, so what the fuck. I could do without all the hymns, though. It feels like I'm working in a mortuary, which might have been a better career path. People never stop dying.
    It's good living alone, but I miss our sleepovers. Of course, you probably miss them more than I do. Remember when I cut your bangs when we were stoned on Magic markers? God, I miss the old days. Call if you come to town. I'm a fool for a woman in uniform.
    Love, I

1/19/75

Dear Laura,

I was most distressed to hear of your recent confinement in an Amsterdam Prison. Tough break. Ever since Rockefeller created that stupid law about going to prison for doing one lousy line, it's taken all the fun out of doing drugs. I'm glad to hear you'll be extradited soon, and will be back in the good old USA. Yes, Woodstock would be a good place to settle, but no one famous lives there now. I hear everyone is out in LA, shaking and baking.

I heard from Ben Morrisey last month, and he's sober now. He married a super model and she's expecting. He asked after your boobs, and wonders if you'd mind smuggling some hash into the country between them when you return. He's willing to pay big.

I'm antsy without a man. Not that I haven't had several boyfriends and lots of sex, but the thrill wears thin after a few boinks, so I've been celibate for awhile. You probably head for the salad aisle when you're lonely, but I fantasize about finding love.

I'm getting tired of radio. I know I have more potential than raising faders. Maybe I'll get into TV. It's not that different, but at least there would be famous guys around to marry. I need a change. It can be a man, a job or a new apartment. All are diversions from my problems, until I get used to them. Then they *become* my problems.

Call when you get back. If you have any appreciable drug residue up your ass, come on over. I'm not picky.

Love, I

DECISIONS, DECISIONS

1/2/75

Dear Arnie,

I began work today at WINZ-AM (all news, all the time, until you're sick of the whole business), and I've already met the hottest announcer. His name is Guy and I want him. Love to you and your new wife, Sandrah. I hate her. I

4/3/75

Dear Arn,

Guy and I finally went out last night and it was ultra-romantic. We had two bottles of chianti and fucked our brains out. I'm definitely smitten. In addition to being really well hung, Guy is a total hoot. Funny, but not overly interesting. Whatever. As long as he loves me I'll be okay. I'll give him two more dates, then I want to hear those three little words—Indian or Sushi? Kidding. It is so cool dating a famous newsman! I feel really validated now. Love, I

7/6/75

Dear Arn:

Guy still hasn't said those three words so I've started seeing Jerry, a writer at WINZ. He drinks a bit and *always* says he loves me. That's the great thing about alkies—they're devoted, even if they have trouble hoisting their flags. The problem is, Jerry's not Guy. He's brighter, cuter, and he's from the Philadelphia Hallorans, but I'm fixated on Guy. I'm going to give him an ultimatum. Either he commits or I'm choosing Jerry. Maybe he'll back away and I'll end up with Jerry without having to make a choice. I hate choosing. I'm *so* bad at it. No matter what choice I make, it's the wrong one. It's hellish being in love with two guys. I want them both. No doubt I'll end up with the one who's not right for me, and down the line it will be too late to rectify my error in judgment. Jerry is everything I've ever wanted but I'll end up with Guy, I just know it. My life is like that. It's how I lost you. By the way, congrats on the birth of your daughter, and gracias for naming her after me. Are you high? Who other than my mom would name a kid after a large piece of real estate? Miss you. I

1/1/76

Arn:

Happy friggin' new year. I'm in hell! I gave Guy an ultimatum and now he wants to commit, but I don't want to give Jerry up. I love them both! I wish I were a cat. Animals have the right idea. They don't need dinner and drinks before they mate, they just do it. (Of course, they eat their young and use their tongues as toilet paper, but no world is a perfect one.) We humans carry around all this neurotic socialization crap and make the same mistakes over and over. It's so fucked! Who says we can't fuck two people at the same time? Who made up those rules? I don't remember casting a vote. I know I'll end up choosing Guy, but not because I care about him more. I'll choose him because he's on the air. I'll regret this in the end and want Jerry back, but he'll probably be with someone named Muffy and I'll be alone again, naturally. You'd think that knowing this, I'd avoid the inevitable by picking Jerry in the first place, but no. I've got to have

Guy. I'm so fucked. I

1/15/76

Arn,

I'm so bored with Guy I could scream primally. We see each other once a week because of his kids, and when we get together we do the same thing over and over—movie, dinner, wine, fuck. Blah blah blah. He can't make me come the regular way so we use the vibrator after he comes, but by then he's no longer into it and could care less if I come, so then I start to feel like I'm boring him, which turns me off and then I don't want to come. He never initiates a conversation, and when I ask a question he never knows the answer. 'I don't know', he intones. 'I just don't know.' For a reporter he's pretty fuckin' stupid. I miss Jerry. He reads the New Yorker and is able to complete the Saturday Times crossword in ink.

I knew this day would come. Of course now Jerry is dating this producer from WBCS. God, I feel so trapped! I've gotta get out of this relationship but I don't want to hurt Guy. Maybe I can *make* him want to leave me. Of course then *I'll* be hurt. Even if I engineer the breakup, I'll still feel rejected. You have your Masters in Psych. How would you describe my behavior? I

2/5/76

Jeez Arn,

No need to be insulting. I know I'm fucked up, but borderline schizophrenic seems a bit severe. Anyway, to add further fuel to your diagnosis, I did the one thing guaranteed to drive Guy away. I fucked his brother Lewis. Not that I initiated it. We were all at Lewis's in Greenwich, and Guy had to leave for work. I missed the last train to the city because we smoked too much Thai stick, so I crashed on the couch. As I was falling asleep, Lewis's wife Annie invited me to sleep with them, and a light bulb flashed inside my muddy Thai-sticked head. Maybe if I slept with them, Guy would find out and split. So I did. Annie did me while I fellated Lewis, and I came twice. Then I sucked Annie's tits and she came. (Does this make me a lez?) Then Lewis fucked both of us and *he* came—in *her*, thank God. I've always wondered about the algebra of the ménage, but it was actually quite a pleasant equation.

I won't tell Guy about this, of course. I'm not totally stupid. But maybe Lewis will. Oh what a tangled web—I

3/8/76

Arn,

Yes, I'm shameless. Yes, I'm on the pill. But even if I had a kid it would look like one of the brothers, so my bases would be covered either way.

Lewis didn't tell Guy so I finally did. I've been wracked with guilt over the whole sordid business. How could I have fucked my own boyfriend's brother? And his sister-in-law? Now I not only feel guilty about doing it but about telling! I'm beneath contempt. You may be right when you say I have some teensy-weensy intimacy issues. Actually, it's a relief being away from Guy. If I'd heard one more 'I don't know', I'd have killed him as he slept. Now I'm free to find someone better for me, someone more like Jerry.

Arnie, you're the only man I've ever really loved. I think it's why I can't truly love anyone else. Love to Sandrah (the bitch) and kisses for India Jr. I

3/28/76

Arn,

Get this! I left work last night and Guy is waiting in the lobby with white roses. Like I'm some sort of virgin. He says he forgives me and commends me for my honesty. I don't want this! Sigh. I

9/3/76

Dear Arn,

I never should have let Guy back into my life. I think he's dating someone else behind my back now. I could have dealt with rejection when it was timely, but now we have to break up all over again, only this time I'm waiting for *him* to make the move. I think I may move to LA and get into television. Lydia is out there fucking her way through the discos, and claims it's a really happening place. I'm tired of New York, I'm tired of guys, and I'm oh so tired of myself. Lyd says LA is a great place to reinvent one self, but what if I create a monster?

I'm glad you've gone into private practice, Arn. I realize we attended a progressive school, but doing pro bono shrinkage while living among the homeless was a bit radical, don't you think? Plus, I was a bit uneasy mailing letters to Arnie Cohen, corner of 34th and Lex. Good luck on the inside. Your next wife, I

SHRINKAGE PART 2

6/18/78

Dear Lyd,

I'm on vacation in the Big Apple! Sorry you couldn't come along, but it's cool that you're on safari with your latest. What is it—Abdullah? I can't keep track. By the way, sorry about the whole Ebola thing. Hope you're feeling better and are no longer bleeding from various orifices. Anyway, since you're not here I called my ex-shrink, Josh, who invited me to his Soho loft for dinner.

"Hey, Josh. Thanks for hanging with me. I mean, you used to be my shrink and all, and most shrinks feel it's unethical to fraternize with patients."

"I don't believe in ethics. They're too confining. Besides, I was only your therapist for five weeks, and we didn't get into any heavy issues, unless you count the stuff about your mother hating you. But nothing really heavy."

"Cool. So where are we eating? I haven't been to Hunan Hideaway in months and I'm dying for Spicy Vegetable."

"Is there just one?"

"One what?"

"Vegetable."

"No, there are twelve, but it says 'vegetable' on the menu, so that's what I call it."

Josh smiled. "Actually, I thought I'd fix us some wine and

cheese. That way we don't have to deal with crowds."

"Uh, OK, though the Hideaway never seems overly crowded—"

"Great! Here's some Chablis. Relax and enjoy. Close your eyes and put your feet up."

Lyd, I hadn't closed my eyes for two seconds when Josh began touching my puss. At first I freaked, but since it hadn't been touched in weeks I decided what the hell.

"Ummm, that feels nice. Ummm—*what the fuck is that thing?*"

"It's a lapping tongue vibrator. Chicks dig it."

"Get that thing away from me! Listen, Josh, I'm not into kinky sex. I mean, I've had a threesome and stuff, but basically I prefer the missionary position."

"Oy, a sexual luddite. Okay, okay, don't freak. Lie back and close your eyes."

"I don't think I trust you anymore."

"Don't be silly, India. I respect your boring sexual preferences. I even understand where they come from, given your dysfunctional family history."

"What history? Can't I prefer mainstream sex without having suffered some deep-seated trauma? Do shrinks have to delve into the limbic system in order to rationalize every situation?"

"Yes. Now close your eyes and open your thighs." (A real poet, Lyd.) There, doesn't that feel good? And it's just my hand."

"Um, yeah, that does feel ni…. *What the fuck is that?*"

"It's a finger vibrator! It makes my hand pulsate just like the real thing."

I pulled down my skirt and headed for the door.

"Why don't you use the real thing, Josh? Are you impotent or something?"

"Jeez, India, what a thing to say to a Jew! The marital aids in my closet are just good, clean fun. You need to loosen up. I guess I didn't do a very good job with you two years ago. You're still really neurotic."

"Thanks a lot! By the way, Chablis is out and Chardonnay is in. And I'm out of Valium. Could I have a scrip?"

"Only if you fuck me."

I raised my skirt and sighed. "Hi, sailor. Is that a marital aid in your pocket or are you just happy to see me?"

Lyd, do we really need guys? Couldn't we just be happy with a little chard, a lapping tongue vibrator and each other? Miss you lots. Me

———— ((()) ————

2/8/78

Arn,

I can't sleep. Ever. I've tried Dalmane, Valium and running into a wall. Now I'm hungover, woozy, and have a nasty egg on my forehead, but I'm still wide awake. I think it's the roaches. They're up all night playing poker and laughing at me. I'm borderline psychotic already. What's next, the Three Faces of India? I've got to get out of New York. I hate yellow snow! I

2/14/78

Arn,

I have no Valentine, only Valium. It's snowing. It' s been snowing forever. I wonder if WINZ health insurance covers lobotomies. How can you stand being my friend anymore? It's so great that you love me unconditionally. Wish I did. Love, I

3/1/78

Arn,

Guess what!!!! WINS bought me out for 15 grand! California here I come! I can't wait. Lydia's gonna put me up 'til I find a pad.

I hear Guy is engaged to some manicurist who he *has* to be smarter than; Jerry says he has trust issues and I'm the reason; and I'm about to move three thousand miles away from my family. Can life get any sweeter?

Congrats on getting your Doctorate, though personally, I feel that getting a hundred and hour for forty-five minute of 'Well what do *you* think?' is bogus. What happened to pro bono work? Couldn't you split the difference? Off to pack. I

3/25/78

Dear Arnie,

I've lived in LA for two weeks, and things are moving at a snails pace. I have no job, eat Taco Bell Enchiritos twice a day (yum!), and Lydia is screwing the actor from that new cop series who lives in our building. I think his two black labs may be involved, but she's staying mum on that issue. Last night I followed Travolta into his garage, but was kicked out by some wetback doorman. All in all I think I'm gonna like it here, once it stops raining. Have a nice day. Rilly. I

TRUTH IN
ADVERTISING

7/15/78

Arn,

Guess what! I've decided to enter the fast-paced world of advertising, just like my dads. The money is great if you get into the right area. If I lie and tell them I have a BA, I'll probably pull down a hundred grand. If I make it an MBA it could be two hundred. Claiming an MBA might be pushing it though, since I only have twenty-four undergrad credits. I could say my MBA is from some esoteric school like Hofstra, and that I got it under my maiden name, but why take the chance? Listing a BA isn't really lying, it's just stretching the truth. OK. So I'll list a BA in Liberal Arts from Hofstra, which was conferred under my maiden name. Wait! I still use my maiden name. I'll have to choose another maiden name. And as long as I'm choosing a new name, I may as well pick and ethnic one to facilitate my job search. How about India Gonzalez? People with Zs in their names get hired first in LA. It's called Affirmative Action. It doesn't matter how smart you are, only how many Zs are in your name. That settles it. I am now India Gonzalez, and I have a BA in LA from HU. Wish me luck!

WENDY VEGA

7/31/78

Dear Arn:

I've had two interviews so far. Here's a taste of each:

"Ms. Gonzalez, so nice to meet you. Welcome to Ritem, Cellum and Rippemofsky."

"Oh, thank you, Mr. Rippemofsky. It's so good of you to see me, you being the owner of the agency and all. I've heard so many great things about your shop and about you in particular. I—"

"India, quit gushing and sit down. You've already gotten your foot in the door. And the name's Sy."

"Thanks, Sy. I hate brown nosing , but my best friend Lydia says it's the way to go."

"Well, there's no need for that here. Now, what school did you say you graduated from?"

I started to freak. I'm thinking, shit, he's found me out. That's why he asked what school I *said* I'd graduated from. Semantics are everything. I began hyperventilating, hoping that if I passed out, Sy would forget the question. Then I began worrying that he'd think I don't work well under pressure. But I *don't* work well under pressure. I hate pressure! Why did I ever think I could make it in this stupid business?

"India, are you okay? You look a bit ashen."

"Oh, it's nothing sir, er, Sy. A little too much jojoba this morning, that's all. That stuff is so unpredictable."

"Tell me about it. I have the same reaction to prunes."

"Oh God, prunes! Don't get me started. My friend Lydia ate so many prunes once—"

"Uh, what say we get down to business. What experience do you have in the ad biz?"

"Well, both my fathers are in it."

"Swell. But why should we hire you here at RCR?"

"Because I'm funny, bright and cute, and I know how to bullshit people?"

Sy looked skeptical.

"Plus, I give really good blow jobs, in case that would be a deciding factor." It wasn't.

Interview #2 went like this:

"Welcome to our shop. I'm Dan and this is my partner, Tom. We hope you don't mind this impromptu audition, but we feel it's the best way to gauge a person's grace under pressure."

There was that nasty P word again.

"Groovy, what should I do?"

"Simple. This is a brainstorming session. You sit in, and if any killer ideas come to mind, feel free to chime in. We're all friends here, and there's some coke on my desk. Today we need to come up with a name for a new product. Picture this—an aerosol foam kept near the crapper, the contents of which you use to, er, clean yourself after you crap. Obviously, we have to pull the curtain on decency here. And keep this in mind. Middle class people will be buying this shit. Rich people have bidets. Any suggestions? Tom?"

"How about Quickleen?"

"Not bad. Sounds like a laundry product, though. I was thinking more along the lines of Afterglow."

"I don't know, Dan. Sounds a bit sexual to me. Let's face it. Shit is not sexy. Yes, India."

"I don't mean to contradict you, Tom, but I did have a fun time once involving feces and a carafe of chianti. Anyway, how about Happy Endings? It's subtle but gets the point across."

"Hey, that's great! But I'm afraid it's too visceral. It indicates a geographical area—you know, your rear end—and might be a bit evocative."

"Well then, I guess No Shit is out of the question."

It was. They said they'd call me, but haven't yet. If they don't, I might consider becoming a shrink like you. I have twenty-four credits already. I'd only have to go back to school 'til I'm middle-aged. Plus, I'd love to move back to NYC. I miss black snow.

So how's DC? I cannot believe you sold your Brooklyn Heights brownstone and moved there. Are you high? Have you shrunk the heads of any famous pols? I want names, neuroses and peccadillos. Fuck ethics. Love, I

SNATCHES

8/7/78

Dear Arnie,

Last weekend Lydia and I decided to do some late-night club hopping. Tired of the Green Chili, we drove around looking for a groovy new disco where we could strut our gorgeous bods. After an hour in Lyd's Le Car, during which she regaled me with tales of her co-worker Hilda, who'd left her husband for a chick, we pulled up to a place called Snatches.

"Let's check it out!" we cried in unison.

After valeting the car, we stuck our heads in. (Valeting is such a scam. I mean, I can see it in the big city where some guy takes your car and deposits it in a secret valet space which exists only in a parallel universe, but in the Valley you pay three bucks to watch some Mexican pull your car into a space you could pull into yourself for free. And then you've gotta give him an extra buck to get it out! There, I've vented.)

"Not bad," I said to the bouncer. "Excuse me sir, is there a cover charge tonight?"

"It's five bucks, and I ain't no guy!" she replied.

Who knew, with those mutton chops? After murmuring appropriate mea culpas, we paid the damages and entered.

"Let's get a table and find some dudes," Lyd said.

And so we did. Find a table, that is. An hour later, Lydia grew restless.

"Ind, we've been sitting here longer than most Hollywood marriages last, and no one has asked us to dance. So, you wanna dance?"

"With each other?"

"Why not? We used to do it in high school."

"True, but I don't want anyone thinking we're lezzies like your pal Hilda. Besides, they're playing a slow number. I'm not dancing it with you, even if you are my closest friend."

"I'm hip. Hey, how come all those other girls are dancing together? Why don't the guys at the bar ask them?"

"I dunno. Let's go over and check out the merchandise."

And so we did.

"Holy shit! Those aren't guys, Lyd, they're chicks! We're in a l-l-l-lesbian bar!"

"Jesus, no wonder no one has asked us to dance. They probably think we're a couple! Let's get out of here!"

But I'd paid three bucks to valet and five bucks cover, and I was gonna get my money's worth. What harm could it do? Besides, I needed another chard to quell the shock.

"Okay, I'll stay," Lyd said grudgingly, "but don't expect me to enjoy myself."

"Lyd, there's nothing to be afraid of—unless your femininity is threatened. Maybe you like it here a little too much, eh chika? Maybe you're starting to think I look pretty good, si?"

"Shut the fuck up. You sound like Olga Dubcek. I'm staying because it's already 11:00, and I don't feel like driving over the hill."

"Whatever. Hey Lyd, that redhead is scoping out your boobs. Oh no, she's coming over!"

"Hi, I'm Brenda. Would either of you hot throbbing snatches like to dirty dance?"

Lydia gagged. "That's it! I'm throwing up right now."

"Lydia, chill. No thanks, Brenda. We're a couple."

I batted my lashes and Brenda lumbered away.

"Jeez, Ind, I heard things like this went on at gay bars, but I didn't know it went on at lezzie bars, too."

"Lyd, lezzie bars *are* gay bars. Let's dance. It'll get your mind off Brenda."

"My mind isn't *on* Brenda, for fuck sake! Okay, I'll dance, but no slow ones."

"Oh come on. Just one?"

"I'm warning you, keep your mitts off me!"

I assured Lydia I wouldn't grope her, and we danced.

"See, this isn't so bad."

"True. Hey, maybe if we pretend we're lezzies, no other lezzies will bother us."

I pulled away with celerity.

"Whaddya mean, like we should make out or something?"

"Don't be gross. I simply meant we should hold each other while we dance, sort of territorially, so the lezzies will think we're together."

"Like this, with my arms around your neck?"

"Yeah, that's cool. Hey, we're slow dancing and I didn't even notice."

"Wow, me neither. Should we stop, Lyd?"

"What the hell. One dance is harmless. At least you won't get a hard-on."

When the song ended we bellied up to the bar for a refill. Lyd pointed to a non-lezzie looking lezzie.

"Wow, check out the chick with the double Ds!"

"You know," I said, " I'm toying with the idea of getting my boobs done. I mean, I work in Hollywood so it's practically a job requirement. I'd never consider enhancing them if I still lived back east. New Yorkers don't care about boobs, just real estate."

"Ind, you were a New Yorker until six months ago."

"Well, I've changed. Too many SigAlerts, I guess. Now all

I want to do is have a nice day."

"Hey, you wanna do our boobs together?"

"Nah, one of us has to be able to drive the other one around afterward. You're not allowed to drive for two weeks."

"Forget it, Ind. I'd go nuts if I couldn't drive. I guess my boobs are large enough."

"Hey, here comes the bartender. God, is she hot! Hi, babe. Two more chardonnays, please. What's your name, hon?" I asked, winking.

"Candy. Two white wines coming right up."

"Jeez, India, were you flirting with her?"

"Sure. She's gay. She expects it."

"But you went there so effortlessly, like you're gay, too."

"I'm not gay, I'm versatile. If I pretend she's a hot guy it's easy. You should try it."

"Here's your wine, ladies. By the way, you're the best looking gals I've seen at Snatches in awhile. You doing anything later? We could make it a threesome."

The idea sounded reasonable. I mean, what the hell—it wouldn't be the first time.

"Sounds like a plan," I replied.

"Ahem, India, may I speak with you privately?"

Lydia yanked me into a restroom labeled Bitches. There was no men's room.

"India, are you out of your fucking mind?"

"Well, we haven't had any other offers and I'm horny."

"Do you have to get laid every Saturday night to make your life worthwhile?"

"Well, yes, since you're asking."

"That's it! We're splitting. I'm getting you out of here before you do something you'll regret."

"Lyd, I already fucked Annie and Lewis at the same time. How much worse is this?"

"Yeah, but there was a guy involved so it wasn't technically a lesbian experience."

I gave in reluctantly and we walked outside.

"Whew, feels like rain. The air is so fresh. Lyd, what came over me in there?"

"It's the herd mentality."

"Thanks for saving me. I was on the brink of depravity and you snatched me back just in time."

"Eeeww, must you use that word? Come on, let's hit the Green Chili. I need a testosterone fix."

"Okay, but save the last dance for me. And remember, being bi doubles your chance of getting laid."

And so, Arn, we got laid by guys that night, after all. I forget their names, but I was thinking of you the whole time, I swear. Besides, if I turned lez I wouldn't want you, and that would be a tragedy. Kisses to Sandrah. On second though, just give her a hug. I wouldn't want to send mixed messages.

Have a nice day. I

HOLDING AND WITHHOLDING

8/15/83

Dear Arnie,

Guess what? I'm in love with the new booth announcer at KNOW. I know, I know, not again. His name is Ben Franklin and he's British. Too bad he has a girlfriend, but I'll remedy that. It's funny. I have absolutely no ambition in any other area, but when I want a man, I become rigidly single-minded. Give me a month and Ben will be mine. Too bad you're not. Love, I

10/1/83

Dear Arn,

Okay, so it took two months. After a drubbing by the LA Times softball team, a bunch of us from the station adjourned to J Sloan's. After a couple of beers, Ben let it slip that his girlfriend bailed and is back in New York. I wasted no time, practically throwing myself at his crow's feet. I guess he got the message, cuz when we got back to my car we made out passionately. He attributed it to the five Dos Equis, and says he doesn't date women he works with. We'll see. Love, I

10/3/83

Dear Arn,

My 33rd (aargh!!!) birthday was bliss. Ben took me to see 'The Big Chill' and gave me a yellow vibrator. After going for sushi, we came home and tried out my gift. He even said he loves me, though he still mentions his ex a lot. It's so great having someone who really cares about my happiness, even if he does a few lines once in awhile. He claims coke makes him more sexual, but that he's thinking of giving it up. That would be nice. I

9/30/84

Dear Arn,

Congrats on your second kid! Even though you had her to save your marriage, it doesn't hurt to have another white, middle-class kid floating around.

I've been with Benjy for a year now, and I'm more in love than ever! It's such fun living together. Of course, there's not as much sex as before, and we fight a lot, but other than that it's swell. Alas, Ben hasn't given up coke. In fact, he's snorting more that ever, but he's so funny I don't care. Funny at work, that is. When he gets home he either ignores or criticizes me, but I guess I deserve it. I *am* self-absorbed. Ben reminds me of this at least once a day, so it must be true. He also accuses me of being overly defensive, which I guess I am, since I'm always defending myself when he says it. I'm so happy I have someone who keeps me in line. I

10/4/84

Dear Lyd,

Thanks for the obnoxious birthday card—great photo of the old woman and her saggy tits. I've never gotten a black eye from jumping rope, but thanks for the warning.

For my birthday, Ben hinted I've gained weight. He's such

a stabilizing influence, always keeping me on track. I just wish we didn't work together. We're always fighting now. Sometimes I think of splitting, but he's so successful and I hate being alone. After dinner we bought some coke and snorted it during 'Carson'. I hate coke, but Benjy likes that I do it with him, because then I can't bitch about his doing it. But I bitch anyway.

"Benjy (sniff), this stuff is so bad for you (snort). You could drop dead (snort) at any second (sniff)."

"Don't worry, luv (sniff), I only get mild angina (snort). Nothing to fret about (sniff)."

Well, in that case... I

5/11/85

Dear Arnie,

Benjy and I were married today! Since we'd already bought a condo to save our relationship, we decided what the fuck. I wanted a large wedding with a long white dress, but Ben had this dream about how everyone in church was laughing at him, and after he awoke hyperventilating, he decided we can only have ten people at the ceremony. Okay, I figure, it's Ben's starter wedding, and I'll do whatever it takes to get him to marry me. Never mind that most of our friends will never speak to us again, or that I won't be able to wear a bridal gown, because I'm sure as shit not shelling out two grand if only ten people are gonna see it. So we had a pleasant service at The Little Brown Church, where Reagan married Nancy. The bride wore Laura Ashley. The groom wore khakis. Afterward, twelve of us came back to the condo, where Ben and I opened our gifts, including some lovely microwave cookware and a minivac. All in all, a nice boring day. I love Ben so much, even if he *is* a bit withholding at times. I'm so happy being married again. Wish you were here. Love, I

5/12/85

Arn,

Paging Dr. Bombay, paging Dr. Bombay. Emergency, come right away! Last night—my wedding night—I dreamed I was fucking a stranger. Somehow I don't see this as a positive sign. Please advise. I

5/23/85

Dear Arn,

You may be right about my dream symbolizing repressed hostility, because I hate Benjy and we're talking divorce. Every time we fight he throws my words back in my face. I'll I say I'm unhappy, he says *he's* unhappy. If I say I'm not getting my needs met, he says he's not getting *his* needs met. I can never have my own feelings. It's like fighting with a five-year-old British kid—they sound intelligent no matter what infantile shit come out of their mouths. I can't believe we married. We're so ill suited! Ben loves coke (but swears he's giving it up) and I hate it. He's moody and negative and hates this about himself, so he accuses *me* of being moody and negative. He never says I'm pretty, only fat. I'm 5'4" and weigh 110. How fat can I be? And the sex could be phoned in at this point. Why can't married people sustain passion? How the hell am I supposed to feel like making love at night when the day has been full of anger and recriminations? Are we supposed to sweep the bad shit under the rug, like we rub the last of the coke into our gums? Still, I need the guy, even if he is a bully. I think I've married my mother—again. I

10/3/85

Arn,

My 35th birthday. Seems like the fucking things are coming twice a year now. I was in a pisser of a mood all day, worse than PMS. To top that off, Ben didn't buy me shit. At least I had another sweet dream last night. I've had them nearly nightly since the wedding. In them, I'm always fucking a stranger and it's always fantastic. I miss casual sex. I should have paid more attention when we tried on our rings before the wedding and I got that icky feeling in my stomach. Now I'm destined to grow old with someone who thinks I'm fat and unlikable. Hey, I may eat a lot, but I eat healthy. All Ben has left at the end of the day are bloody tissues. His other car is definitely up his nose.

Perhaps I'm looking for gratification in the wrong places. Maybe I should have a kid, but I hate the little fuckers. I'm thirty-five. Can I start counting backwards? *I*

12/12/85

Dear Lyd,
Things are looking up. We've met this great couple, Dave and Deena. Dave is a reporter for NBC and Deena is his trophy wife. Dave looks like Gregory Peck, and everyone adores Deena. I can't believe they like us. Our friendship is like a Heineken commercial. I wish Dave weren't married, though. After hanging with him, Ben seems so blah. I need someone high profile. I want someone who earns as much as Dave. I want Dave. Slap me, Lyd. *I*

5/7/87

Dear Arnie,
Welcome back to the Big Apple. Now that Watergate is ancient history, I guess there weren't enough political scandals to keep you busy. Sorry the wife felt like staying in DC, but look on the bright side. Would you really want to be married to a tobacco lobbyist at this point? Now you can wait for me. I'll only be a little while longer.

Dave and Deena are hanging with us more than ever.

Deena keeps saying she loves me (maybe I should slip her Olga's number), and I still have the hots for Dave. Funny thing is, I don't even like the guy. Why doesn't this matter? Love, I

8/8/87

Dear Arnie,

Ben has found someone new! He's known her for two weeks and they're already living together! He's getting a quickie divorce and they're marrying in the fall. How much could he have loved me if he's already remarrying? I'm im-mobilized by grief. I can't leave the house. I can't breathe. Will I never learn? Jeez, all I asked for was a little affec-tion. If that was too much to expect, fuck him. No, I can't say that! I love him too much. Fuck me! Fuck me! Maybe I can learn to expect less. I'll do anything to stay with Ben. Anything! Gee, I wonder what Dave's been up to. Now that I'm single—

I miss you, Arnie. I don't want anyone else. I have too much baggage now. I

4/23/88

Dear Lydia,

It's comforting to know you and I are going through parallel divorces. Maybe we should move in together and pretend to be lezzies. That way I could get on your health insurance. Are you acting like a lovesick fool up there in the Bay Area? Have you parked in front of Louie's new place just to feel his presence? Have you gone to bed wearing his after-shave? Have you visualized him fucking his transitional bitch? God, I can't stand being single. I need a man to be happy! The pisser is, I'm older, pickier and less attractive than I was ten years ago, and so are the men. I'll probably end up settling. Dave and Deena won't speak to me now. I lost them in the divorce, along with the fucking Dustbuster. No offense, Lyd. It was a really great gift. Love ya, me

12/25/88

Dear Hope,

It's Christmas and I'm alone. Boo freakin' hoo. I feel a wee bit silly these days. Here I am, alone on a family holiday, while my ex opens gifts with his newly impregnated wife. I heard through the grapevine that Dave and Deena are having a party right now, replete with a snow making machine, and I'm not invited. What's wrong with this picture? How did I get left out in the cold? Here I sit with my INDIA Christmas stocking and a bottle of Dom, too embarrassed to speak to or write anyone. I think I'm becoming a misandrist. Maybe even a misanthrope. I'm certainly growing weary of myself. Is there a name for that? (Sui-thrope?) It's just that I feel I'm losing control of my life. Every decision I've made has been the wrong one. Men, work, real estate, mutual funds—you name it, I'll fuck it up. I feel frozen and unable to move, because I'm afraid the next decision I make will be the wrong one, too. Meanwhile, Merry Christmas to me, and better luck next year, you self-centered bitch. Me

LYDIA PHONE CALL #2—1987

"Hello?"

"Hola, Lyd."

"India, what's up?"

"Nuthin'. Just called to rap. You busy?"

"I think I'm getting black lung."

"How's the remodel going?"

"Christ, I can't walk into my own fucking kitchen. And now these stupid fucks have hiked the price of re-tiling halfway through the job."

"I'm not sure that's legal. Maybe you should call your lawyer."

"And get this! The older contractor, who's the uncle of the younger one, says he fired his nephew and will have to do all the work himself, so it'll take twice as long. The next day, the nephew comes over and says he's fired the uncle, and claims it's gonna take *him* twice as long to finish. I cannot believe—"

"Actually, Lyd, there *is* something I need to discuss. You know that resume I sent to CBS last week? Well, I have an interview tomorrow and I don't know what to do."

"Ind, that's super! Whaddya ya mean you don't know what to do? Take the job."

"It's not that simple. The job is mixing 'The Old and the

Feckless', and it means working the early shift. I hate mornings. I sleep 'til noon to avoid them. For all I know, they no longer exist. And now I'll have to be in at five AM!"

"You'll adapt. And besides, you have a VCR. Anyway, so I told the uncle—his name is Mustafa—I said..."

"It's not just the early shift that bothers me. It involves working weekends. Only weird people work weekends."

"Thanks a lot! I've worked weekends for years, and you're *lots* weirder than I am. You could teach classes. So I say to Mustafa—"

"Plus, what about my writing? At the job I have now, there's lots of down time. At CBS, I'd never have time to write. And what about the gym? It's always so crowded at night—"

"Hon, these problems aren't exactly up there with Nixon's six crises. *I've* got *major* problems. These two yutzes have supposedly fired each other but they both show up each day, hissing and spitting like cats, and since they each feel they're doing all the work, they're both billing me the full amount! And I can't fire them because I've already paid half. Or is it a quarter? I'm so confused! What should I do?"

"Well, you could..."

"I know! I'll visit my brother in Miami for two weeks."

"Let me get this straight. You're leaving town for two weeks while two disgruntled, possibly psychotic contractors are alone at your place, duplicating each other's work and double-billing you accordingly?"

"Yes. I just don't give a shit anymore. Besides, my hubby will be here. I'm calling the airline right now!"

"I'm also thinking about buying a Lexus, but I'm not sure if I should finance or sell my Romaire Bearden and finance half. What do you think?"

"Ind, if you want lower payments, put more money down. Huh? Oh shit! Mustafa is ripping out the tiles that Homer just laid. He says the work is substandard. Funny, it looks fine to me—"

"If I do use the Bearden money, I won't have any capital left. But if I put it into a CD, will I be able to make back the interest I'd lose making larger payments?"

"Who am I, Alan Greenspan? Call your accountant. Why do you need a new car, anyways? Your Accord is just three years old."

"Yes, but it doesn't reflect my current lifestyle."

"Ind, you only make eight grand more than you made when you bought the Honda."

"*I know* that. But if I get the job at CBS, I'll be raking it in. Hmm, maybe I should wait on the Lexus 'til after I make my decision. If I stay at my old job, I'll need a new car to stave off depression. Staving off depression was *way* cheaper in the fifties. Lucy and Ethel bought hats."

"Hold on. Fuck! These two idiots are throwing grout at each other. You know, they don't look that much alike, and their offices are in West Hollywood. I wonder if they're g..."

"The thing is, if I get CBS, I may not be able to take my vacation to Australia. Do you think they'd front me some vacation days before I start working?"

"They'll probably tell you to take the trip, and while you're gone, they'll hire someone with less agita in his or her life."

"But—"

"Ind, it's all in the hands of Kismet. Haven't you read Shirley MacLaine's books?"

"Yeah, I read the one where she's sleeping in the mountains of Peru with a thin poncho for a blanket even though it's fifty below. Give me a fucking break! I think she hallucinated the whole thing. I don't think she ever left Beverly Hills. I've had several out of body experiences in the Valley, but with all the smog it was difficult looking down. Once, after some killer hash, I saw my body lying face up in a pile of—"

"Spare me the flashbacks. I've heard about so many of your trips that *my* chromosomes are fucked up. So anyways, Jose's going to NYC next month on business, and he's afraid of getting pushed in front of a subway."

"Tell him to buy a shiv. They sell them in Times Square."

"Will do. Uh oh, Homer and Mustafa just disappeared into the master bath. I'd better go check on them. I'll bring a bucket of cold water, just in case. God, I hate LA. The air sucks, the guys suck—mostly each other—and it's so plastic. If I lived in Berkeley, I wouldn't have to shave."

"So should I buy the Lexus or not?"

"Buy it. You only live once—unless you're Shirley. Gotta run. The windows are fogging up."

"Love you, Lyd."

"Love you, too."

Click.

CORA

10/11/87

Dear Lydia,

Jesus called last week. No, not *that* one. Jesus Ortiz. He was my first lay, remember? He's a dentist now. He told me that Tony Messina became a priest. God, how ironic! I didn't want to fuck him when he wanted to, and now even if I wanted to, he can't. Anyway, Jesus turned me on to this great new self-help group called CORA—Co-Reliants Anonymous. You've *got* to come with me next time. Then maybe you won't have to ask Jose's permission every time you go to the gym. You're nearly thirty-eight after all. I'm just sayin'—"

So there we were, a big circle full of issues and tissues, and no one in it was capable of sustaining healthy relationships. At first it reminded me of primal therapy, except no one was screaming or puking. Yet. The meeting began.

"Hi. Welcome to CORA. I've asked Cindy to read the Twelve Steps." (Blah blah blah). "Okay, are there any new members here tonight?"

A few hesitant hands were raised.

"Hi, I'm Seth and I'm Co-Reliant."

"Hi, I'm Althea and I'm Co-Reliant."

Jesus nudged me.

"What?"

"You're new. Go ahead. Speak."

"But I'm not sure yet that I *am* co-reliant."

"Trust me, you are. Now raise your hand."

"Okaaayyyy. Hi, I'm India, and I'm not into labels. Just so you know."

"Okay, folks, the Seventh Tradition says CORA is self-supporting through it's members, so we're gonna pass the hat."

I glared at Jesus.

"Jesus!"

"What?"

"Not you! Why can't you pronounce your name Hayseuss like every other Hispanic? Every time I curse, you answer. Jeez, I can't believe these people want cash. I haven't even gotten anything out of the fucking group and they want bread?"

"India, it's only a buck, and you don't *have* to pay. This isn't EST. You're just cheap."

"I am *not* cheap!"

"Bullshit. You never paid for anything when we were dating."

"I was seventeen, for fuck's sake! Did you want I should fork over my allowance?"

The sharing commenced.

"Hi, I'm Elaine, and I've been feeling really co-reliant today. My husband went on a bender last weekend, and I had to bail him out of County. I'm so tired of being needed. Just once I'd like to do something for me, but I won't. I put everyone's needs above my own. That's why I'm here, so that next time, the asshole can rot in jail, and I can tell the kids to drop dead when they ask for Chuck E. Cheese. And tomorrow I'm buying a doggie door. I'm tired of walking Fifi ten times a day. Fuck her and her overactive bladder. Thanks for letting me share."

"Hi, I'm Brad and I'm co-reliant. I've been celibate for

two years, as you all know. Well, I've finally met this woman named Marci, and I'm totally in love. I feel so strong now, and able to deal with a healthy, long-term relationship. And the good news is, she's in CORA, too! We have so much fun together. Like, the other night we were trying to decide which movie to rent. First she deferred to me, then I deferred to her, and since we couldn't decide, we fucked instead. Later, we got up to go to dinner but couldn't decide where. First she deferred to me, then I deferred to her, then we went back to bed and fucked again. It's all so romantic. And we've decided not to rescue each other anymore. Last week Marci's bike wiped out and I didn't help her, even thought she had a compound fracture of her tib-fib. We're so much closer now. Thanks for letting me share."

"Hi, I'm Rosie and I'm co-reliant. I had a weird day yesterday. I went to Disneyland with three other co-reliers, and none of us could settle on a ride. Finally, we wrote our favorite rides down on scraps of paper and drew them out of my Mickey Mouse ears —*after* we had a drawing to decide whose ears to use. I'm never going anywhere with anyone from this group again. Thanks."

"Hi, I'm Zora and I'm a co-reliant, alcoholic, sex-addicted gambler."

"Christ, she must have a full calendar," I whispered. "Are you gonna share, Jesus?"

"Nah. I'm only here cuz I couldn't find a CA meeting."

"Sort of like Zora, right?"

"Ind, Zora is a meeting junkie."

"But isn't that the paradox of the whole thing? Aren't we just swapping one addiction for another?"

"Not if we surrender to our Higher Powers."

"Jesus, I'm an atheist so this whole thing is a waste of time."

"Don't worry. Once you attend a few meetings you'll start feeling spiritual. I'm not saying you have to get religion.

Your Higher Power could be a tree, or even a Reebok."

"Get real. I'm not surrendering my will to a running shoe. Maybe I should just appoint Neiman Marcus as my HP, seeing as I worship there regularly."

"Yeah, well, I personally don't consider shopping to be a religious experience. By the way, are you going to share tonight?"

"*Are you nuts???*"

"Why not? Talk about how your husband dumped you for a twenty-three year old reporter because he wanted fresh meat. You're old meat, kiddo."

"*Whaddya mean old meat!?*"

"Hey, no cross talk!" yelled Zora.

"Er, sorry, I didn't mean to interrupt. Whaddaya mean old meat?" I whispered. "I have the body of a teenager. Ben loved my body. He couldn't get enough of it."

"And yet he did."

"Uh, hi, my name is India and I'm co-reliant. I'd like to talk about my asshole ex-husband, Ben. He moved out last year and I'm a wreck. I loved him so much. The shithead took all my Liz Claiborne towels, too! He used to be so wonderful, so in love with me. I miss him so much. He's such a dick! He said he wanted his space, and then married someone three months later. He was such a great lover, too. Now he's already gone and knocked up that bitch. How could he do this to me? I hate being alone. I hate the bastard! I'm glad he's gone! Who needs him anyway? I do! I miss him so much, I—thanks for letting me share."

"Okay, group, time for the Serenity Prayer."

Jesus put his arm around me. "See, that wasn't so bad, was it?"

"I feel better already. Can we come back tomorrow?"

"No, you're on your own. But my good friend Sam over there would be happy to sponsor you."

"Hmm, not bad."

"India, behave. You're supposed to be learning to be happy *without* relationships."

"OK. Well, thanks for introducing me to CORA."

"I'm glad it helped."

"Fuck that. It's a great place to meet guys. "

Lyd, I'm not sure yet how *not* to have relationships. Alkies can stop drinking, sex addicts can stop fucking, but how do you stop having relationships? It's inhumane, but I'm working on it. I

4/4/88

Dear Arnie,

I've been celibate for several months, and am now a group leader in CORA. It feels good not to have another person inside my head. Lately, when I've been able to turn things over to my Higher Power, good things have come my way. It's nice to finally be free of men. They were my drug, and I've detoxed. Still, I must always be aware of the addiction. Meanwhile, I don't need the aggravation. Plus, I've seen enough dicks to last a lifetime, and they haven't gotten any prettier—yours excepted. I

VILLAGE FRIENDS – AGAIN

6/3/88

Dear Hope,

Lydia flew in from the coast to accompany me to my twentieth reunion last weekend. It was notable.

"Lyd, thanks for coming with me to Village Friends. Christ, do I need a valium. Class reunions suck. I'm petrified of aging. I wonder what the internal equivalent of Loving Care is. I hope it's chardonnay, but it's probably joy."

"India, you're babbling."

"I know. I should've stayed at this school. No telling what high-powered career I could have segued into from a school like this. Instead, I spent my formative years at James T. Kirk, learning underachievement."

"Well, you met me, so it was worth it, right?"

"Right. Jeez, I hope Arnie shows tonight. We haven't seen each other since his divorce. Wow, everyone looks familiar. Like their parents, only newer."

I spied a frizzy-haired woman over by the crudités, dressed in black leather and double dipping her jicama.

"Hey, Lyd, that's my old bathing buddy, Marci. God, has she developed! Of course she would have, she's thirty-eight. Marci worked her way through all the seventh grade boys.

I wonder who she's with now."

"Judging from the hirsute female companion hanging all over her, I'd say she's off men."

"Oh, here they come—"

"India, you look great, lady! I'd like you to meet my partner, Martina."

"Hey, Marce. Hey, Martina. Attractive outfits. Commited any felonies lately?"

Marci smiled patiently, and I noticed her teeth had been bonded. "So funny I forgot to laugh."

"Marce, didn't I hear you were of counsel to some billionaire in the Bay Area?"

"Yeah, that's how I met his daughter, Martina. We fell in love while I was defending her for pederasty, and we've been together ever since."

As Marci looked adoringly into Martina's eyes and kissed her with tongue, we made our getaway.

"It's not that I'm uncomfortable with lesbians, Lyd. You and I did go to Snatches, after all. But I took several baths with Marci back in the day, and I still have fond mammaries. Who knew she was gay with all those boyfriends? Jeez, no wonder she used to tingle when she washed me."

"Huh?"

Seeing no one else familiar, we walked around the school, taking a nostalgic tour.

"Gosh, it seems so small now, like everything is half scale."

"That's because you're taller now."

"This is too intense. I need another chard."

As we passed the Social Studies room, I noticed a guy in clerical robes standing atop a desk, making disgusting noises.

"Hey, that priest sounds just like Scotty Kent, the grossest boy in fourth grade. Oh God, it *is* Scotty Kent! Oh no, here he comes!"

"Oooh, he's hot," drooled Lydia, as Scotty walked over.

"Hey, Scotty. I see things haven't changed much with you—still standing on desks being disgusting."

"It's father Scotty now. I was just goofing around for old time sake. I'm much better behaved at the rectory."

"That's a relief. Oh, no! There's Neddy Greenberg! One time he stuck dog shit in my desk, and everyone thought I'd made in my pants. I got him back the following week when I barfed on his Keds."

"Why the orange sheet, Ind?"

"Eeew, he's a Krishna! And he's dancing this way! Let's split."

Searching for food to absorb the alcohol, we entered the cafeteria, where I spied Peter Joel, the love of my seventh grade life.

"Lyd, he must be here for this twenty-fifth! Wow, he looks great for forty-three."

"I'll say!" she drooled. If she kept on, I was gonna have to find a diaper. I considered going over and flirting, but Peter had last seen me when I was twelve and had a cowlick. That sort of impression stays with a person, and I knew he'd never take me seriously.

I spied my seventh grade teacher, Blanche, stuffing brie into her maw. Blanche's husband, Marvin, was tried for espionage in the fifties and landed at Sing Sing. This gave our jazzy, left-wing school a further sense of panache. It wasn't until later than I realized how infamous Marvin was, and who his equally infamous married cohorts were. Blanche looked old now—all the teachers did. And I'm sure seeing us scared the shit out of them as well.

Outside in the courtyard, we ran into Lynn and Joan and Amy and Linda and Calleen, and they looked really good.

"God, Lyd, everyone is aging really well. I thought I'd feel old tonight, but it's just the opposite. This is bliss! It's definitely the best time I've ever had without sex, though that would add a nice dimension to the proceedings. Speaking of which, I wish Arnie were here. You'd like each other, Lyd. I can't believe my two besties have never met in all these years. I wonder if we'll ever get together. Still, living with a shrink would probably get on my nerves after the first honeymoon months that occur in all relationships—even those with ax murderers, I suppose."

"'But he's so good in bed, your honor. I don't care if he's whacked apart a few torsos. He's mine and I love him.'"

"Haha! Lyd, you're sick. Enough sentiment for one evening. I need sleep. This has been the most validating day of my whole life, unless you count the day Arnie proposed when we were twelve, but—shit!"

"India, look out!" warned Lydia, as I crashed into someone.

"Sorry, I wasn't looking where I was go—Arnie, it's you! I'm so happy you're here! This is my friend, Lydia. Lyd, this is Arnie Cohen,"

They shook and Lydia turned to leave.

"I'm gonna get lost for awhile. Father Scotty seemed interested, and I've wanted to fuck a priest since 'The Thornbirds'. Nice meeting you, Arnie."

"So how's the head shrinking going, Arn?" I asked, as we headed to the wine station.

"Not bad. Now that I have my doctorate, I charge more. What's up with you?"

"I'm writing a semi-autographical novel and still dating TV people. Fame is the ultimate aphrodisiac, and all that. Anchormen are smoking' hot at work, but outside the station they're about as scintillating as a Reagan news conference. I don't know why I keep falling for the same type, over and over."

"You just haven't found the right man yet. And remember, I made you a promise when we were kids. Here, drink!", he said, shoving a chard in my face.

Oh my god! Did Arnie just repropose? This is so great! I

definitely want a big wedding this time. Now I can get that dress I saw at Kleinfeld's, and we can rent out St. Pat's for the wedding. I've been in LA long enough to appreciate the city again—as long as it doesn't snow. And we could hold the reception right here at Village Friends where it all started, and get Dean & DeLuca to cater! I knew going to this school would pay off in the long run.

"Uh, what promise was that, Arn?"

"Don't you remember? I promised to take you ice skating at Rockefeller Center."

"B-b-but don't you remember that other promise you made?"

"No, sorry."

" Never mind. It's not important."

"Hey, lets go across the street to Figaro's for old time sake. Maybe we'll run into some beatniks."

"Okay, Arnie," I sighed. What the hell. It just wasn't meant to be. It'd been twenty-five years. Of course he'd forgotten his childhood proposal. I didn't want to get hitched again, anyway, and I can go to Dean & DeLuca by myself.

"So India, how would you like your latte?"

"Lots of foam, please."

"Will you marry me?"

"Huh?"

"Will you become my wife?"

"Arnie Cohen, is this some kind of joke?"

"Hell no! I've been waiting years to pop the question again."

"Why didn't you say so in your correspondence?"

"I had to wait until my parents croaked. No way I could've brought home a shiksa, even a half-Jewish one. So, what do you say?"

"Yes, yes, yes! Oh Arnie, I've always loved you, even since you stood up for me in third grade. God, my mom is gonna freak when I tell her I'm remarrying—to Arnie Cohen of all people. God this is so weird. But great. Definitely great."

As we drank our lattes and planned our nuptials, I saw Peter Joel over by the cannolis. God, was he gorgeous, and I've always preferred older men. Okay, I was rationalizing, because suddenly I was scared shitless to marry again. Arnie is the best, but after all these years we were more like siblings. Peter, on the other hand, could really clean my clock. Hey, maybe I can have them both—

"Uh, Arnie, can we talk?"

Just then, Lydia showed up and the rest is history. Love, Me

THE BEGINNING
OF THE END

9/5/89

Dear Lydia,

Greetings from JFK, where I've just been sodomized. Though I can understand the need for tight security, my body cavities are my own, and I don't need anyone snooping around.

Yesterday was so wonderful! I've finally married the man of my dreams. Thanks for being my maid of honor, though at our age, matron might be the more appropriate term. By the way, did you notice that mom wore a black arm band? It was probably a commentary on marriage in general, but still—

Anyway, in case my plane crashes, I'm mailing you this memento of our years together. Consider it my wedding gift to you. It's a look back at my life, but also testament to you and how you've evolved into the wonderful broad you are today. If we make it to Nice, I'll send a postcard. If not, publish or perish. And, remember when...

Au revoir, India

THE END

10/11/2014

Dear Lyd,

Arnie and I recently celebrated out twenty-fifth anniversary, and aside from the usual 'familiarity breeds contempt' bullshit, it's been heaven. Thanks again for slapping some sense into me that night at Figaros (I still have scars), and for taking Peter Joel off my hands. Who'd have thunk he had such a small dick? At least he took you to 21 before you found out.

As for Arnie, now that I'm a successful writer, he's shrinking heads pro bono at a shelter on the bowery, though he may relocate to Flatbush due to gentrification.

I still adore my husband. He's been a rock, he's amusing (if a bit dysphoric), and he can still get it up. I'm so glad we got married, but then, I always knew we would.

Overall, I've enjoyed being a stepmom, but I'm happy we didn't have kids of our own. I could never have faced grandmotherhood. I know you regret being childless, but trust me, you're better off with cats. Tommy and Pickles love you unconditionally, and they crap outdoors. What more can you ask?

I'm glad you're on Matchless.com, but please watch out for ax murderers, married men, and men who crap outdoors. Remember, we're getting our faces lifted next spring, and

WENDY VEGA

we won't get the two for one discount if you're killed.

By the way, look out for my next novel, 'The Dykes of PS 17', dropping in time for Christmas. I've dedicated this one to you. Not that you are one, but I think you have tendencies. See you. India Kelly Cohen

CPSIA information can be obtained at www.ICGtesting.com
Printed in the USA
LVOW12s2243130315

430541LV00001B/278/P